R. A. MACAVOY

This special signed edition

is limited to 500 numbered copies.

This is copy

445

In Between

In Between

R. A. MacAvoy

Subterranean Press 2009

First Edition

ISBN
978-1-59606-264-1

Subterranean Press
PO Box 190106
Burton, MI 48519

www.subterraneanpress.com

This is for Mr. Thomas Keu,
with gratitude
for all the grace
he lent to Ewen Young

May all be happy.
May all be peaceful, and at ease.
May all be safe.
May all be free from fear.
May all know the truth of their own nature.
From The Metta Sutta

$\mathcal{E}$WEN YOUNG LIKED drawing from life. He was good at it.

The drawing that this gallery visitor was now looking at was one of his own favorites. Ewen tried not to look at his drawing, nor at the man, but that was not possible. "I love this," the guy said. Ewen was the closest person about, so he had to turn and listen. "The thing's both a hawk and a man, which is cool, and the man looks like he could be someone in particular. Like a real guy."

"It's Willy. He is a real guy." Ewen pointed to the scrap of paper thumb-tacked under the matted drawing. It said, "The way Willy looks at you." Another potential customer drew up beside them, holding her glass of mediocre champagne. "He looks to me like an Indian shaman in one of those wooden hat-things. That is, if the shaman were wearing a sport jacket." Ewen didn't know if this was a compliment or not, but at least she was expressing interest. That was good. This whole show was going well, in fact, except for the fact he had to be there. He stepped back to allow the two wealthy young people to discuss his work.

In his red silk turtleneck and black jeans, Ewen's trim figure looked utterly comfortable with the gallery scene. He was achieving that look by light meditation and breath control. He would rather have been standing in a pail of ice water. Another woman was regarding one of his larger paintings with such intensity she was squinting. He strolled over, pulled by her concentration. This was another work he liked and of which he almost felt protective. He wondered what this stranger saw.

She spoke to him. "You lead the eye from the rose leaves in the very foreground to the red in the back of the garden and finally to the subject's face. These areas are so cleanly done, I can see the line of shadow from the cloud cutting right across his blue eyes.

"And only after I decide his expression is not quite as peaceful as it first seems do you notice his hand is gripping a wickedly-thorned branch of the rose bush." The woman turned to Ewen and he saw her squint had something to do with the thickness of her glasses. She was not as nattily-dressed as most of the visitors and her hands were stained. "I look at this and want to...to befriend the man. Is that what you felt when you painted it? Is he one of your sister's patients?"

Ewen blinked. "I'm sorry, but have we met? I have a terrible memory for..."

"I'm Enid Buhl. I paint."

Now Ewen blushed and put his hands together behind his back, like a repentant child. "Yes ma'am. You certainly are. You certainly do. I'm sorry I didn't recognize you. How do you know about my sister?"

Buhl shrugged. "Recognize me? How could you recognize me? It's not like we have our photos on the backs of our canvases, eh? And I know of your sister because my husband's in her field. Small world and all that."

"But I've seen a couple of your self-portraits, and they were..."

"Without my glasses. I cheated. Love to do self-portraits—the model works cheap and never complains about the pose."

Ewen, who had started to lose his hard-won cool in meeting this very famous and influential artist, found he was beginning to smile for the first time this evening. It was probably a stupid smile. "I, uh, love your work, Ms. Buhl."

"Enid. I think yours is kinda cute too. Tell me about this one."

"This one" was a very spare watercolor of a nandina bush with a nuthatch hanging off a branch upside down. "That's from my Chinese-American period," he said promptly. Enid Buhl sputtered in laughter. "Okay. Good one." Her eyes, enlarged by thick bifocals, looked at him merrily. "I've been wondering. How did you get called 'Ewen.' That's more Chinese-Caledonian, I'd think."

Ewen ran a hand through his hair. "My parents' idea of a joke. My mother's name was Yuen, so they combined the families with Young Yuen. Ewen Young."

"And you didn't hate them for it?"

He considered. "No. Not since I was fifteen or so. But then every teenager is embarrassed by his parents sometime. I got off easy."

The great painter snagged a cheese stick off a server's tray. "Well, Ewen. I admire your skill with materials. And your vision. Of course, I don't see exactly what you see. It'll never work that way."

"You're right. I don't even know myself what I see," he blurted out, and then was abashed. Enid Buhl didn't laugh. She just shook her head and walked on. Ewen started to feel very good about the evening.

Glory, the gallery manager, was able to tell him there was strong interest in at least three of his paintings, and not the cheapest of them, either. And the drawings were very popular also, though drawing generally didn't get a lot of interest from these shows. Ewen left her to the business. He felt he had done his job by showing up, and now, having actually met Enid Buhl and been told she liked his stuff, he thought it was the perfect time to leave. Grabbing his leather jacket from the rack, he went out into the night.

Outside it was drizzling and dark: a great relief. Ewen drank in the air, which gave out a wet fog from the warmth the asphalt had accumulated, and it was almost like the smell of earth. Rhododendrons were in their last, brilliant display of red, and somewhere close by star jasmine was scenting the wet breeze. He walked down the Redmond street toward the parking lot where he had parked his Saturn. Droplets of rain weighted his hair, causing it to sway with his steps. He knew he was being followed.

There were two of them, quiet-shoed, keeping the rhythm of his own feet. He felt them to be sheepdogs, and with him as the sheep. He looked ahead for the shepherd.

There, in the small deserted parking lot, standing between the rows of cars, he stood. An Asian man, almost certainly Chinese, dressed in a sort of grandiose rayon sweat-suit. He was standing with legs locked apart, hands in his pockets. He was a lot taller than Ewen, and his hair was badly styled. "You are Young," he said, as Ewen halted fifteen feet from him. He spoke in English.

Ewen's ears were tuned for the padding steps behind him, which came steadily on. "Getting older every day," he said. A gust of wind blew rain into his face. "Tell them behind me to stop."

The man in front began to smile. He was very confident. "Why should I do that, Young Yuen? How can I give orders to these others, or why would I if I could?" The man had switched to Cantonese. Ewen's was rusty, but he understood. The two sheepdogs did slow, only twenty feet behind Ewen, and they triangulated with the man with embarrassing dress taste. "Because I don't know why you have a problem with me. Are we enemies? If so, no one told me."

The man slouched forward. "Enemies, Young. Of course we are, as you are your father's brother's nephew. And student."

Ewen made a disgusted gesture with both arms, and hung his head. "Oh, this is stupid stuff! This is the year 2009 and I am a painter by trade. I'm no threat to anyone!"

"Of course you're not a threat, little man. You're a message." He gestured to the two behind him and there was nothing for Ewen to do but run.

Run straight at the man in front. The taller man jumped into side horse stance to meet him and raised a hard punch, but Ewen's diagonal move sent his face skidding just to the left of that fist, and Ewen took it into a lock with both his hands. His momentum carried both himself and that fist behind the attacker, holding the arm behind the man in a neat half-Nelson. They both skidded across the pavement in a circular dance, while Ewen kicked one of the man's feet out from under him. He was holding the man up, now, in between himself and the two others, and the man made an awkward package.

It was Ewen's intention to use him as a shield. He had done this in more demonstrations than he could remember. But the man was heavy, one-legged and squirming, and the pavement was slippery. He shouted "Do you want to see me break his neck? Does he matter to you?"

One of the two shrugged broadly and tilted his head without concern. The other looked from Ewen, to his fellow, to the prisoner, who was cursing in two languages and struggling violently. Ewen heaved up on the trapped arm, turning the curses into a scream. Ewen heard the scream and thought he might throw up. At the same time he felt a tight, sharp thrill in the moment. He saw only the two thugs ahead of him. He felt only the arm being wrenched by his hands.

One of the two turned his back with exaggerated nonchalance and strolled over the shining asphalt back to the street. The other—the one who had shrugged—continued to stare predatorily at Ewen, but kept his place. After an eternal few seconds, he too loped off.

"Let me go," said Ewen's prisoner, as though he held all the cards.

"Now that seems like a stupid idea, since you're supposed to be a messenger and I'm supposed to be a message."

The man tried to turn to look Ewen in the face, which was not a good idea. He stifled the scream and tried instead to stand higher, to relieve the pressure on his joints. Ewen kicked his leg out again and this time the scream could not be stifled.

"Tell me what you want with my uncle?"

There was a pause before the answer. "Ask him."

"What exactly were you planning to do to me, here?"

The tall man snorted. "Mess you up a little. Like I said. A message. Just mess you up."

"Mess me up permanently?" That idea still struck Ewen as an amazement as he asked.

"No. Of course not. Then how could you tell Jimmy Young? It's him we want."

"Why?"

The man looked down at the pavement and sighed. "Ask him, if you don't have an idea. It's all between the Head and him."

"Head of what?"

"Ask Jimmy Young. You don't get anything else from me."

The thrill of the incident was fading, and Ewen felt the dialogue was getting nowhere. "Maybe the police can do better."

"Your word against mine, you stupid Yank."

"Maybe the police will like mine better, Mr. Hong Kong. Are you a responsible citizen? A citizen at all? Legal at all? I'll take a bet you aren't"

"You people should learn that sometimes betting isn't worth it. How're you going to get me to a cop? Use your cell phone? Ask me to stand here while you dial? Just let me go. My leg hurts; you know I can't chase you."

Using one hand Ewen patted the guy down; it was a rough and inexact process, but he did find a knife. No gun. By now he was sick of the whole situation, and he released the man, immediately sending him flying with a double punch to the back. Mr. Hong Kong came down with a wet sound on his belly. Then Ewen did run. ➤

*E*WEN'S HOUSE WAS what the realtors like to call a "jewel box." It was small, had two stories and two bedrooms, and everything within was hand-done, including the old plaster. The artistic perfection of it was marred by the heavy weight bag set in the large entryway, and the clutter, canvas tarp, and smell of paint that dominated what had been the dining room. He had lived in it alone for the two years since Karen and he had drifted apart. That's how he referred to it to himself. "Drifted apart."

As Ewen walked in, he called his Uncle Jimmy. Jimmy Young was still up. Ewen described the assault at the parking lot and asked for explanation. When Uncle Jimmy was finished cursing he gave some mild criticism to Ewen on his technique, which he said had been haphazard and indecisive. That done, he admitted that Ewen had survived these mistakes, and said he believed he knew what enemy was responsible. What enemy school was responsible. He was no more forthcoming than that, but then this was not unusual for Uncle Jimmy. He said he would have a talk with someone. He said he might get a restraining order, but even if he didn't there would be no more trouble anyway. He suggested not going to the police. So often the police can't tell the difference between the bad guy and the good guy, and Ewen would then be under their eye. It wasn't good to be under their eye.

Ewen was not happy about Uncle's idea of "having a talk." He also knew just how useful restraining orders were. Uncle Jimmy told him not to worry. He told him to go to bed. Ewen needed his sleep. Uncle Jimmy needed his sleep.

Before hitting the sack, Ewen paced awhile, then went into the other bedroom, where there was no bed but only a small table and a round pillow with a mat under it. On the table was a small plastic Buddha, of no particular lineage, and a small painting out of Ewen's early period. His childhood period, actually. Twelve-year-old period. It was of his mother. He bowed to both. "I avoided a fight, Mom," he whispered. "You'd have been proud of me." He then crossed his legs and lowered himself onto the pillow, put his hands together at head level and bowed once more. "I take refuge in the Buddha," he murmured. "I take refuge in the teaching. I take refuge in my family, and I take refuge in the great family."

He sat until the events of the night—both the nice and the nasty—fell into perspective, and then he went to bed.

Mrs. Lowiscu didn't understand why she had to get up early for her sittings, why there were so many of them and why it couldn't all be taken care of in a few long bouts of painting. Ewen had explained that it had to do with lighting, that he couldn't do it like a photographer with floods and reflectors, and that her children themselves (who were paying the bill) had chosen the light into which granny should be shown. By the time a family had gotten old enough, numerous enough, and wealthy enough to desire and afford a portrait of grandmother, grandmother herself was also of an age to have opinions. It didn't bother Ewen, who got along with old people and got up very early anyway. Nothing bothered him unless his subject couldn't sit still.

Mrs. Lowiscu sat as still as a sleeping snake, and Ewen hoped that recurring image of her did not implant itself into his work. Her face itself was very rewarding to paint, for the olives and roses of her original coloring had been aged into something touching on purple and ash. Complicated. Challenging. She had chosen a dress of mauve, which was decades out of fashion but had obviously meant something to her at some time in the past, and Ewen slid that color subtly into pink, to make her old cheeks more lively. Her old dark eyes he left alone.

He drove to his sister's workplace by ten and parked in the tiny lot beside it. The front garden was filled with flowers and fern, all of it light and airy compared to the almost black rhododendrons in boxes before the offices on either side.

Pacific Rim Help House had really been a house years before, built in a pseudo-Wright style. It was still a lovely building, though the glass made it hard to heat. The young woman at the antique Chinese desk glanced up from her computer screen. "Lynn," said Ewen. "Here for Lynn."

The middle-aged receptionist responded at though she had never seen this man, who came in at least twice a week asking for his sister. "Dr. Thurmond is with a patient," she said. "Would you like to leave a message?"

"No, Caroline. I'm Ewen, Lynn's twin brother. If I put a wig and a dress on I could probably fool you into thinking I *was* her. Like every other time I show up, I don't want to leave a message. I'm supposed to be here. Look at your schedule." He reached over the desk and pushed the little spiral binder toward Caroline. "Look. Please tell her I'm here."

The receptionist, evidently alarmed by the invasion of desk-barrier, retreated on squeaking chair wheels. She made placatory gestures with both hands and, as a last line of defense, asked Ewen to be seated. Instead, he strode through the tiny, empty waiting room and through the door which was painted in ink with a galloping horse.

Inside Lynn's domain was the smell and sound of running water. A section of the paneled wall had been replaced with a rough wall of sandstone, down which the water ran, collecting in a small pool with goldfish, into which someone had thrown pennies. Both the horse-door and the fountain wall were of Ewen's making.

Lynn looked like her mother. Most people remembered this when they saw a picture of Lily Young, but as Mrs. Young had died twenty years ago, the resemblance was usually remembered only by Ewen, who was a painter and had a gift for faces. And who was a son and brother.

Lynn wasn't with a patient; she was in her office with a tall cup of Starbuck's tilted up against her face. She was making guzzling noises. As she heard her brother open the door, she lowered the cup guiltily.

"Just what every psychiatrist needs," she said. "A good caffeine jag."

"If it works for you," he answered. "So—what is it? Is it Jacob again?"

The two did not really look that much alike, except in face and expression. Lynn Thurmond looked as though a breeze could blow her over, while for Ewen Young it seemed that it would take a category three hurricane. But some smart-aleck in high school had taken to calling them "The Smiling Anime Twins" and, the name had stuck.

She nodded and with a Kleenex dabbed off a latte mustache, careful not to smear her lipstick. "He's biting himself again. He asked for you. Are you up for it? I mean after last night?"

Ewen had been swinging himself into one of Lynn's armchairs and stopped in place. "What do you know about last night? Do you mean the gallery?"

"No. Uncle Jimmy called me this morning. Told me to be careful. Which was big of him, don't you think? To deign to tell me I ought to be careful because he's got himself into something nasty? That man has got some stuff in him!"

Once again Ewen was placed between Uncle Jimmy—his teacher—and the rest of his family. "Oh, I don't know, sis. It takes two to make a fight, but only one to make a massacre."

"But you're not hurt, right? I'd know if you were hurt. I'd have woken up."

"I'm not hurt. I skidded a strip on the side of my new tennies, that's all. But I'm here for Jacob, so let's see Jacob."

Jacob Fischbein did not look like the sort of boy that would be biting himself. He looked very normal, healthy, even athletic. This last was true, for Jacob was a wrestler at Redmond High, and it was in uniform, on the mat, where he had stopped being able to hide his unhappiness from the public world.

Lynn and her brother entered the special room in which there was nothing with which a person could hurt himself, unless by paper-cuts. Jacob sat with his feet up on his cushioned chair, his elbows resting on his knees, hiding in his own darkness. Defending himself with his own darkness. He looked up at them warily and began in his usual way.

"Hi, there Doc. Hi, Doc's brother. Spare me some change? Mind change? Change of venue?"

Ewen said nothing, but looked in the corners for a cushion. He found two, both of a floral pattern, looking like fat Hawaiian shirts, and he dropped them in the center of the room. He sat down on one, legs crossed, and dropped the other one down in front of him. Ewen was not smiling at the boy's brittle wit. He was tired and he knew he was going to work, but he gave him a comradely glance. He dropped his hands loosely into his lap and took one deep breath. "Okay. Let's sit down, Jacob." He closed his eyes.

He heard the shushing of the boy's Levis. There was a small noise as Jacob's baseball cap sailed over the room and hit a chair. That trick with the cap was a sign of respect, thought Ewen. Respect in Jacob-language. At that he did start to smile. He reached out, not with his hand. For the first moment of the touch Ewen was a bit afraid—afraid of Jacob's fears and of Jacob himself. Afraid of the effort involved in opening. Then he just did it. He opened.

A small space of damp grass, surrounded by trees. Some of the trees were maple and some were evergreens. To the left was a low wall of stone—limestone—he could taste it slightly. Beyond that was the smell of water. This was a place Ewen had found a long time ago. He scarcely remembered where. He did not know what it meant or how it was that he could get there, but he was now the keeper of it. He felt the bounds, he marked them and fortified them, and now he allowed the mind of Jacob—a bad storm, a bruising wave, a maddened dog, a child—to enter.

Ewen let him in and closed the gate behind him. He defended the borders of this small place that was no place at all. That was Ewen's whole job here. Keeping the borders.

The Jacob-storm entered, hit and howled against the immaterial walls, but even the branches of the trees weren't bent by it. The wave of Jacob's misery struck against nothing and it vanished. The biting dog, the biting, the always-at-the-edges fear-filled biting found nothing to bite. Ewen held within his mind this small, open place where only the boy sat, sat gripping the grass in his fingers, sitting tight as a drum. Ewen himself did not enter in with Jacob. This was Jacob's refuge. In a sense Ewen *was* the place, and in another sense he wasn't part of this event at all. Ewen's place-making was a huge, simple concentration, just at the limit of what he was able to do, but Ewen sat on the pillow, unmoving, and he kept the boundaries.

Lynn was shaking his shoulder, gently. He felt himself flinch.

"How are you?"

Ewen opened his eyes and squinted at the light. There was Jacob on the carpet in front of him, his head on the other Hawaiian pillow, sleeping like a baby. "I'm tired," said Ewen. "I am really tired today."

The tiredness went away after five minutes pounding on the heavy bag. Ewen was now angry, as he had not had time to be the night before. Angry at the Hong Kong idiot with the bad sense of drama and the bad haberdashery. Angry at the sheepdogs behind him. And, yes, really angry at Uncle Jimmy. No way around that. Now that there was no one in the family to defend him against, Ewen was thinking Uncle Jimmy every kind of horse's ass. He remembered the matches, one after another through his childhood, which he had had no choice but to compete in. No choice but to win. The classes for which Sifu James Young had never showed up, and which had devolved upon Ewen—who had to show up because Sifu James Young might well not. Always without pay, because he was family. Well, of course *he* never had had to pay for his training, either. He hadn't *had* to keep going. Mom hadn't been hot about the whole martial arts thing at all. From her he'd gotten the other sort of art. Dad would have backed him on dropping out, even though Jimmy was his brother. Especially because... Lynn never felt obliged to follow kung fu. She'd been more the ballet type. The pony club type.

Ewen had done it all to himself. Be honest about it. He was still doing it *to* himself. Who was he fooling? He did it because he was good and he knew it, and because... because it was grand.

He worked out for forty-five minutes and then once again he was tired, but not in the same sense. He took a shower and went out to putter around in the garden.

Ewen's kung fu curse was Uncle Jimmy, but his garden curse was bamboo. He didn't dislike bamboo in and of itself, but for what it had done to his four years dwelling in that small, suburban house. Ewen's grandfather had liked bamboo very much, and had planted different kinds of it all over the back garden and the front yard. He had not been too informed about the care and growth-habits of what he had planted, but the stuff had flourished. God, how it had flourished, and so had begun Mr. Young's feud with Mr. and Mrs. Kelly on the right hand side of the property, who had no love for bamboo at all.

For years Mr. Kelly had run down errant shoots of bamboo with his lawnmower and Mrs. Kelly had dug up the monstrosities coming up in her annual border. They had blamed this on old Mr. Young, who had first been of the opinion that the Kellys were fortunate to have such graceful volunteers for their very artificial and ordinary backyard. When resentment grew to fury and the county was called, Grandfather had a service come and dig out his lovely bamboo, and he felt he had done more than his duty toward neighborhood peace. The next year his bamboo came back livelier than ever from its severe pruning and so did the Kellys'.

When Ewen inherited the house he had no idea of the firestorm he was entering. Even though he was not the man who planted the damned bamboo, the Kellys despised him for it. Despised him and all his doings. He found broken eggs on his car hood and once on his windows. The Kellys' German shepherd had him marked for destruction.

Ewen had read some books, gone out to the edge of his property, and dug a ditch three feet wide and five feet deep. In doing this he used nothing more complicated than a shovel. It took him almost the entire first year of his residency, it strained his relationship with his roommate Karen, and did not improve the looks of the street one bit. But when the ditch was done he went to Home Depot and bought rolls of very long aluminum plating and lowered them into the ditch, riveting them together as he went, so there was a metal wall five feet deep separating the Young property from that of family Kelly. It should have been enough.

Bamboo, however, does not always send its runners in straight lines, and some had spread to the yard of Mrs. Blick, behind them both, and Mrs. Blick did not pay too much attention to her own backyard, so now the Kelly's were angry at Mrs. Blick also and twice as furious with Ewen.

These days Ewen would wait for the Kellys to be out, on the rare occasions they took their dog with them, and he would vault the five foot fence in between the backyards and yank out any sprouts of bamboo he saw, hoping to eliminate the problem before they noticed it. He was also investigating the uses of RoundUp.

This afternoon Ewen was in his front yard, weeding around his little water garden. The shubunkins followed him from side to side, poppling the surface of the water with their hungry little mouths and hoping. Ewen didn't notice them. He wanted to call the police about the attack in the parking lot. He had no feeling for the Chinese school vendetta. That seemed to him a custom more fitting for an alien planet than for Puget Sound. Maybe those guys the night before had *been* space aliens. He hoped Uncle Jimmy hadn't degenerated to feuding. Uncle was, with all his faults, a good guy, and had been Ewen's teacher since Ewen was five years old. But Uncle Jimmy was undoubtedly getting crotchety, and being at odds with the rest of the Young family was doing his mood no good.

Ewen believed the family trouble had all started because granddad hadn't approved of his oldest son becoming a martial arts teacher. Not that he hadn't approved of the discipline itself—he hadn't faulted Ewen for taking lessons, and was even proud of the boy when he had won his little boyhood awards. It was just that it wasn't a way to make a living. It had no future, unless one was intensely practical and had good business sense, which ruled out Uncle Jimmy. Better he should have been a lawyer or a dentist. Ewen, unlike Granddad, knew that being too impractical to run a profitable kwoon meant Uncle Jimmy would have been hopeless as a lawyer. Or a dentist. In Ewen's own, semi-practical mind, he was a bit grateful for Uncle's outlaw status, because it made a grandson foolish enough to be a painter seem like a paragon.

He was going to 'handle' the situation? How? A duel to the death on a Seattle rooftop? Paying a hit man? Oh God! Ewen sat back on his heels. He whispered "I take refuge in the Buddha. I take refuge in the *dharma*. I take...A phone call. I take a phone call."

Ewen sprang to his feet, running for the door, because he knew it was his sister, Lynn, and he knew there was more trouble.

"He called Teddy over the schoolyard fence and he said... he said he should buy white clothes, because his family was going to go into mourning."

"He said Teddy's family was going into mourning?"

"Yes, Ewen. Teddy's sure that's what the man said! I called Uncle but there wasn't any answer. I had to leave a message!"

Ewen's stomach turned over. He dialed Uncle Jimmy himself. There was no answer. He got into his Saturn and drove.

He reached his sister's house and darted under the three-color, Tibetan style doorway. He frequently referred to his sister's family as his 'Sino-Tibetan relations' because of Theodore Thurmond's strong Tibetan Buddhist presence, though Theo was a six-foot tall balding blond of

German ancestry. Theo was out on the porch now, face strained, his long blond hair escaping its ponytail and hanging around his face. "We can't get hold of your uncle," he said. "The police are on their way."

Ewen swept by him and banged open the screen door. In the living room was Lynn, hugging six-year-old Teddy, who was two-thirds the size of his mother. They both looked lost. "I'm so sorry," said Ewen, who knelt down by the couch and tried to fit them both into one large hug.

"As though it's your fault," said Lynn reprovingly, with a little snort. She frequently acted as though she were much older and more experienced than her twin brother. It was probably a result of her medical training.

Ewen began to pace, from the big screen television at one end of the room to the altar at the other. "I should have called the police at once. Not just Uncle Jimmy. I should have known better."

"Who could have thought?"

Teddy lifted his head from his mother's embrace. "Is this like in the movies? Where one Chinese guy tries to kill another because of kung fu?"

Lynn patted her son and said absently "No, dear. They have things like the Pride Fighting Championships for that now."

Hearing that simple statement, Ewen stopped in his tracks. Perhaps Lynn really was older and wiser than he was. "You're right. The idea makes no sense. Uncle Jimmy doesn't even have much of a school! That can't be what it's about, really."

"It's about his gambling, of course," said Lynn with a shrug. "Uncle Jimmy must have been having another losing streak."

"Oh." This idea hit Ewen like a brick to the head and he simply stood still for a while. "And that's what the guy meant about me being a message? About some people betting on the wrong things?" He hit his head with the back of his hands. "Yeah. You're right, Lynn. And it would have been no good to break the old man's back, right? Then he could never pay. But a nephew. Or a niece."

"Or a grandnephew." Lynn mouthed the words over Teddy's head.

Ewen denied that forcibly. "I don't think that's what the guy meant. If he had wanted to hurt Teddy, then…Hey, why aren't the police here yet?" He lowered himself into the antique chair opposite the couch—the one Theodore could not use because it put his knees to his chin.

"But you're right about the gambling thing. He gambles a lot, doesn't he? I never heard about it, exactly, but…"

Lynn gave him a look of long-suffering. "Ewen! Uncle Jimmy gambles endlessly, and on anything, from Mah Jong to the ponies to a fly on the window. Why do you think he's always in debt? Why can't he afford a decent studio for teaching, or some equipment made after World War Two?"

"It's because he doesn't charge much," said Ewen reflexively, and then stopped himself. He was done defending his uncle. "How come I never heard this—about how much he gambles? I'm the one closest to him out of all of us."

"That's why, stupid. Dad doesn't want to break your faith in your dear Uncle Jimmy, who gave you so much of his time and attention. And...well, really, he *was* good to you. And you were so good at it. So Dad told you that the reason Jimmy got stiffed in the will and you got the house was because Granddad didn't approve of his career. As if! He didn't want to give away a house that would be immediately lost in a poker game."

Ewen's mind was racing and going nowhere. He was out of his chair and pacing again, and then heading for the door. "I'll be back," he said. His sister bounced to her feet and followed, taking him by the arm. "Ewen, the police will want to talk to you."

Gently he freed himself. "Yeah, when they get around to it. Meanwhile, I'm going to find Uncle."

Theodore was still watching on the porch. Ewen sprang past him and over the stairs. Behind him he heard Lynn's voice, louder this time. "Ewen: stop and take a breath. A deep breath."

"I'll take several," he said, but kept running.

Uncle Jimmy's neighbor, Madge, told him she didn't know for sure where Jimmy was but probably he was out at The Garage. The neighbors still called the place "The Garage," which was what it had been years before, when he had rebuilt it into his martial arts studio—his kwoon. It still looked more like a garage than a school.

Ewen took out his cell phone and tried him at his work number, receiving only the answering machine. He got back into his car and drove the short block to the studio. The single, rolling garage door was locked down, but the small doorway to the side was cracked open. There was light within. Ewen wanted to discuss some things with his uncle. He was perhaps becoming too angry—angry at his whole family for keeping him in the dark, for treating him with kid gloves because he was a "sensitive artist." But he was especially angry at Uncle Jimmy, for making all this deception possible. For maybe endangering little Teddy. He wanted to burst the door open and shout for his uncle, but his long training had taught him discretion in the practice hall, so he quietly opened the door and walked in.

There was the mirror on the wall, the wing chun-style dummy, the heavy bag, the speed bag, the row of striking pads for the adult students, and the tiny set for the children who made up so much of Jimmy Young's clientele. There was the red rubber mat for throwing and falling, and on the mat was Jimmy.

Ewen's uncle seemed to have just accomplished a break fall: one arm flung out, one leg bent up. It took a moment for Ewen to make sense of what he was seeing, and as he did his nose registered a burnt smell. "Uncle," he cried out and ran for the splayed form on the mat, where red had blended in with red.

He knelt on the rubber mat and lifted Uncle Jimmy's head, where there was a small neat hole above one ear and another, worse, below the other. There was a dark, wet spot on the front of his green polo shirt. Jimmy Young's eyes were open and drying.

"No!" shouted Ewen, holding the head as though it were something very delicate: something he could hurt or help by the holding. "No!"

The mirror was in front of him. He saw his own body in it, holding Jimmy's body. His own head, tilted up like that of a keening dog, looked entirely foreign to him. For a moment he saw the angle only as a painter sees things, a shape removed from personal meaning. He also saw something else—the image of a tall, burly, black-haired man he remembered bringing down on the asphalt not twenty-four hours ago. Mr. Hong Kong. Mr. Hong Kong was holding a gun. His nose was bloody. Ewen knew he hadn't hit that nose the previous night. He turned just in time to see the man's eyes narrow over the short sights of the revolver, and to feel a blow to the body that knocked him back over the corpse of his uncle, and to hear a crack like close lightning. Then he knew nothing for a while.

He was walking through a huge hall, or something much like a hall, and there was a light before him: a bright light. It did not seem to be a particularly friendly sort of light—not a very human light—but somehow he knew it. The glow of the light roused Ewen's outsized curiosity, and he wondered how he could express that light on paper. On each side of the light smaller lights were hovering, and in them he saw familiar and comforting things—houses and flowers and people talking, and these flickered with smoke like that of a hearth-fire. He had no doubt how to paint these. He stood amongst them all—the single unwavering illumination and the pockets of comfort—and he tried to decide which was more worth investigating, when a voice filled the place.

It was a familiar voice. He remembered he sort of liked that voice, though he remembered little else, and he tried to make out what the voice was saying. This took some time, during which the soft smoky fireplace lights grew more and more attractive. He felt he was a bit tired and would like to sit down by one of those fireplaces. Then he made out some words.

"Ewen Young, child of a noble house," it said. "Child of the Way. The time has come for you to seek a path. At the ending of your breath, the radiance of the In-between has become visible. This is the essence of reality, the luminous void, the undefiled mind, centerless and abounding. Recognize this, for it is your true state, and rest in it. I will instruct you further."

The voice was Theodore's, of course and this was his version of the introduction to the Bardo. Ewen had heard it.

It was Theodore's own translation, and he was proud of it, so Ewen had heard it more than once. More than necessary, to his own opinion. He had always thought it very wordy.

Ewen looked at the luminescence, the smoky lights and the featureless space through which he was walking. He turned around and suddenly the whole situation seemed very funny to him. He felt an urge to laugh, but restrained himself from politeness. He spoke up. "No thanks, Theo. I don't believe I'll be going this time. But thank you for your good advice. I appreciate it." Then he did laugh, and the great open space broke up with that noise.

Ewen woke up to great pain in his chest, a faint smell of burning, and a number of faces gathered around. There was his sister and there was Theodore. There also was Dad, who lived in Santa Barbara. For a moment he wondered where Mom was, but then he remembered she had been dead twenty years.

As he should be, if he remembered correctly. He thought about this, and wondered how long he had been unconscious. He looked around and met the eyes of his sister.

"Oh, Ewen," Lynn cried. "I knew you'd come back." She touched him.

"Ouch," said Ewen. He passed out again.

That day, Ewen Young entered the world of morphine. He found it a very rewarding one, although nasty pain still got in the way. The sun shone into the hospital room window in the most beautiful fashion, much more paintable than the great illumination he had just left, and the plastic bedside water jar was an entrancing shade of red. So was the lipstick of the nurse. He told her red was a wonderful color, and she smiled in a knowing fashion. "That's the dope. Does great stuff with colors. Don't get to like it too much." Then there was sleep again, and the pinch of the IV line as he turned in the bed, and after more sleep a man in a suit was standing there, clearing his throat. Ewen attempted to speak to him and the attempt really hurt.

"Sorry about this, Mr. Young, but you really should thank your lucky stars you're here to hurt. They almost lost you. Used the paddles twice or so I'm told. You've even got burn marks on your chest."

Ewen gazed at the man and in a thread of a voice asked for more morphine. The man, who was tall, dark and angular-featured, smiled as the nurse had smiled and then he nodded. Ewen closed his eyes and soon the nurse was injecting something into the IV line. He hoped this would erase the pain, but it did nothing right away.

"I'm Detective Petersen of the sheriff's office. I'd like to ask you a few questions, and it will have to be now because in a few minutes you'll be out again. Okay?"

Ewen found he could move his neck easier than he could inflate his lungs, so he nodded and mouthed "First tell me what happened."

The man gave a brooding frown. "You don't know what happened? You don't remember anything?"

Again Ewen mouthed words and hoped the man was good at lip-reading. "I know I was shot. In the chest. I can't breathe much."

"You were shot with a .38 which nicked your heart wall—or membrane or whatever they call it. In fact you can say you were actually shot in the heart. That's a story few people have to tell. You bled half out, went into shock, and your sister and brother-in-law found you. Your heart stopped in the ambulance, and then on the table. Both times it started again. You must have quite a heart, Mr. Young."

Ewen tried to smile but wasn't sure it had worked. His gift of stupid humor rose unbidden and he found he was whispering "I try to be nice to people." He had actually made some sound. The morphine was making itself known.

"Did you see who shot you?"

"Oh, yes."

Detective Petersen lifted his hands to heaven and his brooding face went light for a moment. Then his manner returned to somber. "I'm sorry, but do you know that your uncle was shot, too?"

"Yes. I found him. He was already dead. Just newly dead. I think the same man did it." Now Ewen had a ghost of his real voice back.

"We can pretty well guess the same gun did it, so odds are good. What can you tell me about this man: was he white, or...or Asian, or..."

"He was Chinese. Not American-born. Not from the north. Hong Kong. He was tall: not as tall as you. Big-boned, stocky. He has two bruises on his back and a sore right arm. Also a bloody nose." Ewen's enthusiasm for description outran his breathing capacity and he lay panting.

The detective stared open-mouthed. "Who the hell are you, Mr. Young? Sherlock Holmes? Johnny Smith?"

"No. But I met the guy the night before. He and two other men tried to assault me on the street."

"Tried?"

Ewen didn't have energy for the whole story. "I ran away," he said, and in his present state it seemed a marvelously clever thing to say, and not entirely a lie.

Detective Petersen looked at him long and hard and Ewen could see he was no man's fool. "And you called the police?"

Ewen shook his head and tried to look properly remorseful. "I thought of it, but what could the police have done? I had never met any of the guys before."

"The police might have shown you a lay-out—mug shots, I mean. But probably, to be fair to you, they wouldn't have. Not if you weren't hurt. But the lay-out'll happen now; just you wait."

"I will wait right here," said Ewen, and closed his eyes on the detective.

This waking, seeing faces, and falling asleep again was getting old. Once it had been his sister, and she told him she had known immediately when he was shot, and called 911 from her house. Ewen had no doubts, for when Lynn was in labor with Teddy he knew because he was sitting in the back office of the kwoon doubled over with cramps. It wasn't supposed to be like this with fraternal twins, but so it was. Lynn and Ewen, the smiley Anime twins. She was trying to hug him without actually touching at any point when he fell asleep again.

Then came his father. Dr. Young looked more angry than worried, but then that was Dad. It wasn't his fault; he was who he was. They didn't say much.

It was night when he woke again, this time needing an attendant's help to turn to use the urinal without dislodging the IV. He tried not to ask for the morphine because he wanted out of this particular fading and shifting reality, but his resolve didn't last very long. His heart hurt.

He called up from his mind a vision of Kuan Yin, the bodhisattva of compassion: she of the great heart. In his mind, as always, the face shifted to that of his mother. But after less than an hour he rang the bell and asked for morphine again. They were willing to give it to him.

In dream he returned to the place he had been so recently, the luminous place. Theo was telling him all about it—telling him not to be afraid of the light, and he wanted to tell Theo that he *wasn't* afraid of it, but just not ready to dive in yet. Then he was touring the place, where the dead people drifted off to the sort of light that most attracted them and which determined their next births, and he was wondering how to portray what he saw in oils without using the old Tibetan style which never much appealed to him, when he became aware of noise in the hospital room. There was a nurse's aide clutching to his bedrails, her eyes very wide. "Mr. Young? Ewen! Why did you feel it necessary to tear that IV out of your arm? And where did you leave your bandages?"

Ewen stared at her, uncomprehending and bothered. The shade of the dream was still with him. "I didn't go anywhere. I didn't tear off anything. I went to sleep," said Ewen, irritated. As soon as she stalked off, threatening to tie his hands to the bedrails, he slept again.

In the morning they gave him an ice cube for breakfast, which was fine with Ewen. He was not hungry. A different aide took his temperature and blood pressure, and this one seemed very pleased by the results. Ewen basked in the sense of having passed a test without studying for it. As he became able to think a bit, he remembered Uncle Jimmy was dead, and began to be sad: not only for the loss of his teacher but for the belated loss of his own innocence. That he, of all the family, should have not known of Uncle's problem. Problem—hell, fatal flaw. If someone had let him know Uncle Jimmy was a compulsive gambler, perhaps he could have had some influence, could have prevented things coming to this. Or more likely, he reflected, he could not have. And perhaps he was coddling himself in assuming he hadn't known. There had been all those teasings "I bet you fifty cents you can't kick the tennis ball before it hits the ground." Or "You better win this match because I'm betting on you!" Could Uncle Jimmy have really been betting on Ewen's little kid tournaments? How bizarre. Good thing that he had done well. Usually done well. If he had known he was the object of money, he would surely have blown the whole thing.

As he was thinking on this, the detective of the day before came in, this time with a shorter, blond fellow. Each of them was toting what looked like a big photo album.

"These," said Petersen, "are lay-outs. And I'm going to lay them on your bed. No, don't raise your head; we need you alive for this."

The blond man shot his partner a reproachful glance. "Don't worry, Mr. Young. I'm sure you're entirely out of danger."

Ewen almost laughed. "Sure. Unless this same guy sneaks into the room and shoots me again. Like on TV."

"Not likely," said Petersen, deadpan. "We have better scriptwriters." He opened a book and held it above Ewen's head. "These are men who match your description and have sheets in the Seattle area. Asian men."

"Tall Chinese man is what we're looking for," Ewen corrected the detective, who in turn looked skeptical of that very concept. "This might take a while," said the other detective.

It took approximately three minutes. "That's him," said Ewen, lifting his unencumbered arm to point. "In fact, it looks more like him than most photos look like their subjects. I'd have to say that's a great likeness."

"Hah. And spoken by one who knows about painting likenesses," said the tall detective, surprising Ewen considerably. Then it occurred to him that detectives do research.

"So, who is he?"

The detective winked. "Tell you later," he said, gathering up his albums. Both detectives seemed very pleased. On the way out the blond turned and said "God bless you and keep you, Mr. Young."

"Thank you," answered Ewen. "And—uh—you too!"

That was a very stupid thing to say to the guy, thought Ewen once he was alone again. He felt embarrassed. "And—uh—you too."

He did a small fraction of his usual morning meditation, which was difficult, on drugs and flat on his back. He kept thinking what a stupid response that had been to the blond detective. "And you too!" He kept thinking of how he hadn't known or tried to help Uncle Jimmy. He occasionally was visited by images of Kuan Yin. Or was it his mother? His heart hurt.

Despite the air conditioning in the station, Rick Petersen had the window by his desk wide open. Gideon Ryde, who had no window, had wheeled his chair over and was writing on a laptop, his head resting against the window sill. The day was so beautiful that both men occasionally stopped and stared out at the sun, mesmerized.

Gideon Ryde spoke. "Hey. D'ya think we'll get him, Rikki-Tikki-Tavi? The shooter?"

"Don't call me that, unless you want to get called 'Giddy Ryde' again. And yes, I think we've got Chow."

"It's just Young's word. And things can get complicated when it's among the Chinese."

Petersen snorted. "Ewen Young is about as Chinese as I am Indian."

"Yeah. S' what I said. I mean," added Ryde. "It can get complicated."

Mr. Blundell was not having a beautiful day. He was, in general, a worrying man and not one for beautiful days. He did, however, take a certain pleasure in the attitude of the employee standing before him. Chow was sick with fear.

"Young Yuen is alive, yes, if being hooked up to things that breathe for him is alive. He is just parts, now. No problem."

"Just what? Parts? Parts of what, may I ask?" Blundell rolled his soft desk chair around behind the desk, as a standing man might pace, or a tiger stalk. Blundell chose to wheel.

John Chow knew his English did not confuse Blundell. His English was better than Blundell's, because he did not have the American accent. He knew he was being mocked, and there was nothing he could do about it.

What he did not know was that his boss thought Chow's "English" accent was phony and stuck-up, as though he thought he could convince people he was a Brit and not Chinese at all. These two men could, by merely speaking the same language, offend each other all day long.

"Parts for other people, Mr. Blundell. He is dead for all he means to us."

"So is Jimmy Young, Chow. Dead as a doornail. Where does my forty thousand dollars come from now? Do we ask his brother the cardiologist to pay us back? Perhaps we just pass the hat. You are familiar with the expression—pass the hat?"

Chow was not, but his fear of his boss was giving way to anger. "You know why I killed old Young. He was ready to talk. And the nephew, too. He could have recognized me. Now there is no one who can recognize me."

"Goody for you," said Blundell, lacing his hands over the paunch which concealed the muscles of his stomach.

"Goody for you, too," answered Chow, and he left the room, almost but not quite slamming the door behind him. Blundell watched him go, and for him the day was still not beautiful.

Ewen was sitting up, and the effort this took made him crabby. He tried not to show his crabbiness to all his visitors, who were telling him what a lucky man he was to be alive. He thought he might have been a luckier man if he had not been shot. He was also depressed at the thought of the long time of recovery awaiting him and how weak and flabby he would surely become before it was all done. He had never even broken a bone before and didn't remember a time when he had been weak and flabby. He hadn't known how ego-involved he had been with his body. Well, he was. So there. And on top of everything, he had missed Uncle Jimmy's funeral. Perhaps that wasn't such a bad thing, really.

None of these things did he have to say to his sister. Lynn could read the set of his eyebrows easier than another might read a book. With Theo, Ewen had to be more careful, especially since Theo had done his best to lead Ewen through the bardo, and Ewen had been rude enough to refuse and turn back.

"You know what the doctor told us this morning, bro?" asked Lynn, and then answered immediately, "He said that you have the blood of four different people in you. Five, including yourself."

Suddenly Ewen felt plural—more than plural—his blood vessels carrying a throng of genetic messages like the messages on telephone wires. Sometimes one could hear other people's phone conversations, like wind, behind one's own. Back when they were children they had occasionally entertained themselves with this flaw in the phone line. Now Ewen himself had become a party line. This struck him as being more interesting thought-material than the constant refrain of his luck

"I wish I knew who they were," he said in his thready voice. "I wish I could..."

"Thank them?" ventured Theo Thurmond. "Of course you do. But when they gave blood they already knew..."

Ewen interrupted him crossly. "No. I want to know them for my own sake. To know what—I mean who—I'm made of."

"That you never will," said Lynn, peacefully. "Or maybe, those foreign parts of you are all you ever *will* know about yourself. But I don't think we can find out for you. I'll bet there are privacy restrictions."

Ewen wasn't satisfied by this. Privacy restrictions concerning his inner self. Why did he meditate if not to confront such restrictions? After a few more minutes his people went away, but he thought about his immigrant blood for another hour.

That night Ewen found it hard to sleep; every position was equally uncomfortable. When he did sleep he dreamed immediately.

He was in a small apartment with a glass-doored balcony. On the walls of the apartment were pictures of a small dark child: studio shots, collages, snaps tacked to the wall. This was a very exact sort of dream. On the floor were scattered toddler's toys, including a red-wheeled pull toy shaped like a wooden caterpillar, complete with bouncy antennae. The door to the deck showed red geraniums in pots on the rail and a small bamboo in a pot in the corner. Some vague feeling of responsibility for the bamboo led Ewen to unlock and open the glass door, and once he was out on the balcony he began to be worried that the geraniums on the rail might fall, because the apartment was quite high up.

A passerby might be killed if one of the pots fell and struck him on the head. Ewen moved to put one of the plastic pots on the floor of the balcony but could not move it. A second glance showed him the unit was firmly attached to the rail by a bolt with a thumbscrew. He walked back into the living room, and there was a woman standing in the hall beside the living room, her robe clutched tightly to her bosom by one hand. She was a dark-skinned Asian woman, or perhaps half Asian and half black. Not someone he knew. Suddenly the wrongness of his being there struck him. He lifted both hands into the air in a sign of surrender. "I'm sorry. I didn't mean to intrude. I'm dreaming...I won't hurt you."

The young woman flattened herself between Ewen and the door to the other room. She hissed, "Who are *you*! Who *are* you! How did you get here?"

"I'm Ewen Young," he said, with the cold calm of dreams, but doubting this *was* a dream. "I don't know how I got here. I should be in the hospital." She threw the photograph of the child at him, but it made no impact.

The apartment and the woman went away. Ewen awoke crying out, his heart beating like thunder. The nurse's aide rushed in and berated him once again. Only half understanding her, Ewen looked down at his left forearm, where the IV had been tethered. There was nothing there, and no sign the needle had been torn out. The IV tube lay in a coil on the mattress next to him, in a small damp spot, which was not bloody in the slightest.

"If you have to go so bad, you just let me know! Even if you don't want anybody to watch you, I can just put the can in your hand and leave the room. And if it's...something else, well we can work that out. You're just hurting yourself this way!"

Ewen caught his breath. "I'm sorry, ma'am. It isn't that. I don't think it's that. I had a nightmare."

"A nightmare in which you tore out your IV line?"

Ewen showed his left forearm. "It doesn't look like I tore it out, does it?"

She examined his arm, and then the end of the IV line, lying in its bed of limp tape and damp sheet. "Well, you're not bleeding, at any rate. But if you don't stop this, they *will* tie you up."

Ewen sank back onto the bed: very, very tired. "No, they won't," he said, and mumbling to himself he added, "I don't think they'll be able to."

She snorted. "So that's the word of the great kung-fu master. 'They won't be able to.' You'd be surprised." She left the room before Ewen could explain that that wasn't what he had meant.

He wasn't sure what he had meant. "I got no time for this on top of it all," he mumbled.

The next morning there was a lot more pain. Ewen, abashed, asked for more of the morphine but that was over. They gave him pills. They also took out the IV line and allowed him to put on a robe, so he could start to get out of the bed. It seemed strange and unfair that only a few days after they had told him he had been shot in the heart, or into the wall of the heart, which must be close to the same thing, they were now asking him to sit up and put his feet off the side of the bed, and telling him that soon he would be standing by himself.

Soon he would be going home, they said. This made him feel trivial as well as in pain. When his sister came in he was in another bad mood, which she already knew.

"I brought you something," she said. "Something to play with." She was wheeling that something behind her as a flight attendant wheels her luggage. It was in a big blue suitcase.

It's a game, Ewen. A computer game. I use it with a lot of my patients." She didn't wait for a response, but pulled over his over-bed table with one hand while she unzipped the bag with her other. "It's fun. It works on biofeedback."

"I'm trying to avoid all feedback from this bio at the moment," he grumbled, trying to maintain his attitude of grumpiness in front of his twin. It was not possible. She placed a small computer screen in front of him and began plugging things in to big metal boxes which she laid out on the floor. "It'll be fun; believe me." When he still looked unconvinced, Lynn put on a look of mock-severity.

"You're not allowed to goof around any more, Ewen, because you have been officially declared a delog by Theo's Tibetan advisors. You've got to act impressive.

"A delog? God! What's that? Uh—it isn't any kind of god, is it? Or thing like that? With blue skin and lots of eyes and...and maybe flies out of its body at night...? Please tell me it isn't."

"Not a god. Not even a tulku. A delog is just one who has returned from the dead. Without being reincarnated, I mean. And it's always for a reason."

He looked at his sister uncertainly. "And *you* believe that, Lynn?"

"Well...It's certainly true that you were technically dead. And you aren't now. And of course I believe there's always a reason. For everything. Just it's usually too complicated a reason to understand. Sooo..." Through her obvious weariness, her grin was still shaded with mischief. "My brother the delog. Like the title of a TV show."

"Fine. From now on I'll sign my paintings Ewen D. Young. They'll call it my post-revolver period."

He actually *was* in a better mood when he began to play the game.

It was fun. He could work his skin galvanic response and heart rate variability and a few other buzzwords from his sister's world with nice facility. He wondered if this had anything to do with his ability to exit the hospital bed in the middle of the night. He wondered if he dared share this experience with Lynn. If there was anyone on earth he could talk to, it was she.

But no. She was a shrink, after all, and now she was saying she was sure he could have done better in the biofeedback if his body was not fuddled with drugs. Definitely no.

Ewen continued on, opening magical doors and freeing a falcon from a cage, and was still trying to shoot a computer-generated bow without hitting one of the computer-generated yaks on the hillside when it was noon and they gave him red Jell-O. "Cheer up!" said Lynn. "It could have been green."

Later, while he was alone and still playing games with the machines there came a heavy thump against the door and Ewen started. The door swung open to reveal his father, Dr. Young, shuffling backwards through the hall by the bathroom and then into the room as he laboriously turned a small tree in his arms. It was miniature: gnarled, complex and very beautiful. It weighed a lot. Dr. Young stepped toward the bed, peered around the shrubbery at the bedside furniture, which was cluttered with computer and bio-feedback equipment, and at the windowsill, which was far too narrow for the pot. At last he dropped to one knee and set the thing on the floor. One hand braced against his lower back and he turned to his son. "Birnam Wood to Dunsinane hath come." He said.

Ewen was still goggling, and beginning to shake his head from side to side. The movement became faster. "No. Dad! Don't let that be what I think it is. Don't let it be for me."

Now that Ewen was suitably distressed, Dr. Young felt free to return to his more usual cool equanimity. "Yes, it is for you, and you should feel very honored. This thing—I mean this beautiful bonsai—must be at least as old as you are. Hell, as old as I am."

"I know," said Ewen, shrinking under the blanket. "And I will be its slave for the rest of my life. Why, Dad? Why would you do this to me, sick as I am?"

This banter was what Ewen and his father used to replace intimacy. They exchanged no intimacy.

Dr. Young seemed positively jovial. "Me? Have more respect. This is from your uncle's kwoon. I guess it is actually more in memory of James, but you're the official caretaker. Now don't go on about it. Think what this must have cost!"

"I know what it must have cost. And you know: the care they need is like that of a newborn child—only they never grow up. And Dad, Ryan Watanabe's father raises these things. Which means Ryan Watanabe's father is going to know if I let it die. I'm sunk." He did sink, back onto the bed, breathing with difficulty.

After a moment, he revived enough to ask, "So, what'd *you* get for me, Dad?"

"Two nights without sleep," said his father. "And a lot of prayer. Why—what should I get you? What do you want? A real, gray elephant? A new girlfriend?"

Ewen winced at the old joke. He felt his family believed he had taken a vow of celibacy. He felt they were wrong. Then he had an idea, totally outside the relationship box of Ewen and his father.

"I want something more difficult, Dad. But only you can give it, and I'd really like it."

Dr. Young looked wary. "Go on."

"I'd like you to forgive Uncle Jimmy."

Dr. Young's face went stormy for a moment, then slid into its usual smoothness. Ewen, the painter, did not miss either expression. "Of course I forgive him," said Dr. Young. "He is dead! Do you think I could hold a grudge against my dead brother?"

Ewen dropped his eyes from his father's. "I think it's possible. I'm not saying you hold grudges especially, but..."

"Yes, you are," said Dr. Young. "And maybe, yes, I do. It's hard that you ask that of me: after this violence he led you into, and after all those years of our trying to cover for him. And paying his debts with money that should have gone to you and your sister's education..."

This information startled Ewen. "I didn't know anything about the money. But we got by. We got by real well."

Ewen's father placed himself firmly in the visitor's chair. "We got by only because you were not really interested in education."

Ewen was outraged. "So what's a BFA?"

"Trade school," answered his father, with mischief.

"Ewen, your mother and I worked like horses. And before all that work could make a difference—before I had time enough to give her the life she deserved—she died. All the while James..."

"Also worked like a horse. Sweated like a horse. Do you think a Kung Fu teacher sits back and lets his students feed him peeled grapes? I'm eternally sorry about Mom dying—everyone says I feel it too much—but I don't think the money mattered so much to her. She loved life; she was young, and she wasn't looking to slow down and rest. Uncle Jimmy didn't cause Mom's cancer.

"And as for me, do you think I've been training all these years instead of studying medicine or law because I'm lazy, too, or to act out adolescent rebellion? So I could win fights with other kids, or pick up big, gold-colored plastic trophies?" Ewen found his breath had let him down again.

"I never quite understood your dedication to fighting—especially since you don't seem to be the fighting type. You seemed to be under James's spell, somehow. We saw you as innocent. Almost gullible. I admit now there were good things we didn't understand about James, just as there were...other things about James *you* didn't understand." Dr. Young stood beside his chair, with the heavy-shouldered attitude of a bull beset by spears. His shoulders lowered.

Dr. Young stood up again, slightly alarmed. "Ewen, calm down. You're not so much better you can afford to race your heart like this. I'm sorry if you thought I believed you to be lazy. I never, never, believed that you were lazy. Or rebellious. Or not too rebellious, anyway. You were always a good kid. Too serious about this spiritual stuff, maybe. Maybe just a little too unworldly. So is Lynn. You both got that from your mother's side of the family."

This was an old complaint. It was true May Young had been the only real Buddhist in the family—until her death and the changes it caused—but Ewen had to think of his mother's mother and her restaurant chain, and only with difficulty managed to keep his face straight. Easily he calmed down and listened.

"I will work on forgiving my brother."

The nurses were amused by the busyness of Ewen Young's hospital room. Usually when so many people came to visit, it meant a person was on the edge of death. They were glad to believe this was not the case with Ewen Young. He was just a popular guy.

Of course, the police detectives were in a different category. There was a lot of conversation in the staff room about the shooting, Ewen's very close escape, the murky background of the attack and possible association with mysterious Chinese villains. One orderly on loan from Gastro suggested that Ewen Young himself was a member of a Tong or was even a snakehead. The nurses stared him down.

"Irwin, do you have any idea what a snakehead is?" asked the Floor Nurse. Irwin had only the vaguest, but he wasn't about to admit that.

"They're...they're slavers." When the staff continued to stare, he added, "White slavers, I mean."

"Well, that lets out our Ewen," replied the nurse, and the subject was closed.

Inside that busy room, another biofeedback game was going on, with Ewen and Lynn sharing the finger sensors. Ewen himself was becoming an expert at the game, despite his shortened breath, but when he played with his twin, they were masters.

"Of course, you've played this before, Lynn," said Theo, who was despite himself a little envious.

"Not as much as I should have," answered his wife in a cool, detached voice. "Always too busy." Her eyes were half-closed, and her mind was somewhere within the game "event."

"We're all always too busy," added Ewen, in the same tone. They were making it rain in the game, and the sound filled the room. Then the two familiar detectives entered the room and, with reluctance, Ewen saved the game with task uncompleted. The other three visitors were not at all reluctant to see them, for they had only dealt with these detectives once before, and the police were, to Lynn, Teddy, and Theo, still exotic.

"I'm glad to find you all together," said the taller one. His voice was very deep. "But perhaps it would be better if the little boy went out to play for a few minutes."

"I'll watch him," added the blond detective. "We don't want to frighten little Theodore with talk about…the crime."

"Our son knows about death," said big Theodore, standing boldly. "He knows I run a hospice."

Little Theodore looked from one grownup to another, vastly amused by this interchange. "I *could* go out and play," he stated hopefully. "Or you could go out and I could play the computer?"

Everyone smiled. Theo sat down again. Gideon Ryde sat down on the floor next to the boy, wrinkling his suit jacket. Rick Petersen remained standing. "We've got some more photos, these of people we have reason to believe worked with Chow. We'd like you to see these now, because we plan to move in on the guy today and it would be a help in holding others if you could identify any of these. Don't speak unless you're sure, of course, but if you *do* remember these faces from anywhere…"

Little Ted asked Petersen loudly, "Are you an Indian? I don't mean like from India, but a real Indian?"

Petersen winced and swayed a bit, his thoughts cut off. Ryde leaned over and stage-whispered to the boy, "Yes, he is an Indian, Theodore. But he doesn't like people to talk about it. Especially when he's discussing important things."

"Being an Indian is important, isn't it?" Teddy asked the room at large.

Ewen took the plastic-sleeved photos and examined them closely, hoping to take the attention away from both parties to the interchange. "I don't remember any of these, and I'm usually pretty good with faces, because of doing portraits. I look at faces as possible projects. That's how I see Chow, as a possible...hey!"

Ewen had looked up: not at any of them in the room. He looked intent, then concerned, then alarmed. "Chow! No." After a moment he raised one hand and pointed it at the air. "Wait!" In another moment he vanished.

He was there and then he wasn't there. There was an empty bed, with the covers still lightly sinking down. There was silence, broken only by the squeal of a gurney going down the hall and Detective Ryde sliding up the wall to his feet. Then little Ted stood up and bounded to the side of the bed. "Wow, Uncle Ewen! That's neat!"

For a slow count of five, no one else in the room spoke. Ted turned to his father. "I bet you could do that, too, Dad. If you wanted to, I mean."

Ewen had been here before. He had been here always. The luminosity, undifferentiated, complete, was before him, and he could step into it because that was simply his nature. But as he regarded it, he remembered the shape of his life so far, and it did not seem to be finished—also, he saw another shape beside him. This shape was everything the light wasn't. It was fear, it was anger, and it was ugly. It emitted, like darkness, a fog of desire to push away— to push away from everything. In this strange space it seemed to recede in all directions. Ewen looked at it with his painter's eyes and saw a flower withered in bud, the sepals gone hard and the petals thick and frozen. He recognized it as the man John Chow, who had shot him. He could have drawn Chow in both forms, the angry man or the hardened bud. His immaterial fingers twitched to do that.

Now he saw more—he had a distant vision of Chow himself being shot. It had been in the head, as he had shot Uncle Jimmy, after Uncle had been badly wounded from a distance and was no more a threat. And for an instant, Ewen even saw the face of the man who had shot Chow. It was a pale face, and smooth, and slightly red about the eyes. Then that face was gone. The distant vision was gone.

The thing before him was not Chow anymore, not man nor bud at all, but a force of rejection which moved willfully away from the light and toward a darkness which had not been in the great space before: a darkness it created as it traveled away.

Ewen's thoughts were cool and removed, but he felt he was witnessing a great, cosmic mistake: one which he could perhaps rectify. He went up to the thing which had been a man and said, "No need to do this. No need at all." It turned to him and for a moment there was a shadow of Chow's face, which met Ewen, or whatever he saw as Ewen, and it recoiled in terror. The Chow-thing began to spin away faster, creating confusion where it went. Ewen turned away to take a breath, or something like a breath, to avoid taking in this contagion, and then he turned back again and followed the thing.

He spoke. "It's all right. I've been here before, and it's all right."

"I thought you were dead!" screamed the Chow-thing.

"I—I was dead and you are dead now. It's all okay. Don't—don't spin out of control. Don't be afraid. Come back where you were. You'll find there are better places to go. I was there. It's okay."

Chow closed harder. "Sure, and you just want to help me. Sure you do."

Ewen shrugged his shoulders. He felt no anger. No attachment at all to this situation, but merely a distant compassion. "Why wouldn't I? You're dead. We all die, friends and enemies. That ends being enemies. Believe me—here I am not your enemy, and I don't think I *could* lie to you. Not here." Ewen paused and thought. "I'm sure Theo would say that. Theo's my brother-in-law. He'd say that being afraid or angry is the only thing that can do you damage here. Or maybe just refusing to see clearly. I'm no scholar but I know that much." He pointed back toward the luminosity, which was fading in the distance. "Come back with me."

"You think I believe you! Like I believe this whole thing is happening? Go to hell!" He jetted away toward darkness and a confusion that made Ewen's eyes hurt.

"Wrong thing to say," murmured Ewen. He went back to the ground luminosity, warmed his hands in it, gazed a moment and said to it, "Not yet. Not yet."

The five people in the hospital room had reacted in their individual ways. Little Teddy Thurmond had begun to understand this had not been an action expected out of Uncle Ewen by the rest of his family. Ted's father was chanting, his face slightly pale. The blond detective in the corner was also praying, different prayers. Lynn was still sitting on the bed, looking intently at nothing, listening with her head tilted—it seemed—to something no one else could hear. She did not seem upset by her brother's disappearance. The tall detective was watching with the rest of them, his face alert, composed and waiting, when Ewen came back

He was sitting where he had left, with his gown rumpled up. He looked into each face intently, one by one. He glanced down with a sudden fear that his hospital gown had not come back with him. When finally he spoke, he was careful with each word. "Please tell me what happened here—in your own eyes. Tell me what *you* saw."

Again it was young Theodore who spoke. "You went 'Poof!' Uncle Ewen. You weren't there. Then you came back."

Ewen thought about this, licking his lips. "Was I gone long? No, I can see by the way you're all standing that I wasn't gone long."

"So where were you?" asked the tall detective, quite calmly.

"I was…in-between…" Ewen wrinkled his nose in a thoughtful manner, trying to explain.

"Uhh…What can I say? I was there before, when I was shot, but I didn't take it seriously. I mean I didn't think other people could notice." He sighed in thought.

"It's not a place like this is. Get Theo to explain. He knows more. But—" and he looked at Lynn with some satisfaction, "this explains why the nurses have been so upset with me. They thought I'd been tearing out my IV and walking around." Lynn just shook her head.

Theodore, though, was ready to explain. "I *thought* this was what had happened. Ewen was in a bardo realm—he must have learned how when his heart stopped those times before, and yet he still came back. He came back from the bardo. Actually, all realms are bardo realms, in-betweens, as Ewen said. Life's a bardo. The next life will be a bardo. But the bardo we usually think of, is that in-between life and death, or more exactly, between life and another life…"

"Okay. Thanks," said Petersen shortly, with a curt slash of one hand. Theodore shut up, in between words.

"Life is strange," said Petersen. "Washington State is strange. King County is especially strange. We can't go anywhere with that right now. Before you went 'poof,' Mr. Young, you said Chow's name. What did you mean by that?"

Ewen took a long, labored breath and sank back against the headboard. "It was Chow who went 'poof,' Detective. He's dead. I saw him. As I said before—been there, done that. I thought I could help him. I don't know why I bothered. But he wouldn't listen to me. He ran away—went dark. Where he went, I wouldn't follow. Not for Chow, I wouldn't."

Gideon Ryde stood very close to Ewen, shouldering Theo aside. "Where he went? Where he went? You *saw*, Mr. Young? You saw him go to hell?"

Ewen attempted a laugh. "He told *me* to go to hell, Detective. That was the last thing he said."

"But you didn't."

Ewen's strained smile faded utterly. "Not so far."

Petersen simply repeated, "Chow is dead?"

"Yes, sir. Just now."

Petersen took out his cell phone and dialed. Getting no reception, he strode out of the room. Gideon Ryde followed. At the door he turned back and put an envelope in Ewen's hand. "I meant to mail this to you, but since we're here..." Then he, too, was gone.

"I want this kind of thing to stop," said Ewen. "I wasn't made for this kind of...of..."

"Spiritual travel," said Theo firmly. Ewen nodded and let that description stand. He opened the envelope and stared. At last Lynn asked him what it was.

"It's a sympathy card," said Ewen. "For Uncle Jimmy."

Late the same afternoon two things of note happened; Ewen had a scan which showed his heart was healing very well, and John Chow's body was found dumped in a parking lot by Quest Field. He had been executed by a bullet in the back of the head, just as he had executed James Young.

Detective Rick Petersen entered Ewen's room as Ewen was eating dinner: real food. "Good thing for you you're in a hospital bed in the middle of a busy hospital," he said in his very deep voice. Ewen looked up, chewed and swallowed. "You mean you found Chow?"

"Exactly as you said. Killed about the time you pulled your vanishing act. Tell me, just for my own satisfaction, Mr. Young. Did you kill John Chow?"

"No." Ewen had been expecting that question.

"Did you have any hand in his death?"

"No. Not unless he was killed because you were looking for him."

Petersen smiled slightly. "And would you be willing to take a polygraph test? Purely for *my* satisfaction, of course. I can't really demand it of you."

Ewen looked pleased at the prospect. "No problem. If it were Lynn you were asking, the polygraph wouldn't mean anything, I bet. She's a psychiatrist and uses all these biofeedback programs in her practice. She probably knows how people fake them, spies and such. But me—I only started doing that biofeedback stuff in the hospital, in a computer game. I'll do a lie-detector test for you, but I think you'll have to bring it into the hospital, and I don't know what the bandages around my chest will do to it."

Petersen shrugged. "I have no intention of putting you on a polygraph. I just wanted to know what you'd say."

"I think it'd be fun. And I am very bored. I'm thinking maybe tomorrow I can go home."

The tall man looked doubtful. "I wouldn't depend on it, Mr. Young. It isn't three days yet, and you went flat line twice. And of course, disappeared once."

"Three times, I think," said Ewen thoughtfully. "Disappeared three times. Twice to the in-between and once to some lady's apartment. The nurses keep accusing me of pulling out my IV and going to the bathroom by myself. I swear I never did." He met Petersen's impenetrable eyes. Suddenly Ewen grinned. "You have to understand, detective; the only reason I'm not knocked flat on my ass about all this supernatural stuff is that I'm already flat on my ass. Not used to being weak as a kitten. Not yet used to being still alive. But whatever is happening to me, I think I'm gaining control. Maybe next time I can keep my clothes in order. Drag my IV behind me into the otherworld. Better yet, maybe it'll never happen again at all."

"Some people would really dig it," said Petersen. "Popping in and out between worlds."

Ewen shuddered. "Scares the shit out of me."

Petersen gave him a tight smile and then glanced back toward the door. "But don't get your hopes up about going home tomorrow. You might be disappointed. And if you *do* go, please let me know first." Petersen paused a moment. "I mean, if you go somewhere other than in-between."

"I know what you mean," said Ewen, and he returned to his dinner.

Lieutenant Kopek dropped his hand on a pile of the papers which covered his desk. "Another of your *hunches*, Petersen?"

"Well, yeah. Just a hunch."

"And the hunch told you to contact the ME's office in case a body matching that of John Chow turned up. Just two hours before it *did* turn up."

Petersen slid his weight onto one hip and looked calmly into the lieutenant's blue eyes with his dark ones. "Think, Lieutenant. Assuming James Young was the original intended victim—and I think that makes all kinds of sense—and assuming it was his gambling got him in trouble—and according to the family *that* makes all kinds of sense—then his death was a bad decision. Very bad, from a lender's point of view, as he can't now make his payment, whatever it is."

"The threat to his kid—I mean his niece's kid—wasn't sensible, either."

Petersen stood, imperturbable. "Yes, it was, Lieutenant. It's the follow-up that wasn't. That's why I thought Chow—the guy whom two people identified as Ewen Young's assailant—had blundered. Blundered so badly he had become a liability. So it made sense he would be eliminated."

"The guy *whom*, *whom* blundered," repeated the Lieutenant, narrowing his eyes at Petersen. "What a gift for words! Just like Shakespeare. Well, you're the poet, aren't you, Ricky? According to Ryde, anyway. The literary man." Kopek gave Petersen a look of complete malice. "And aside from your inspiration, I suppose there's no private source of yours to go with this hunch?"

Petersen shifted his weight again and looked at nothing in particular. "Sir. If there was a source to this idea...it was not of this world." He snickered as he said this, to make it sound like simple sarcasm.

Petersen had not needed the reminder. He disliked the lieutenant, and he despised the way Kopek mocked his part-ner. But Petersen was sensible. He didn't envy the lieutenant or want the lieutenant's job. What he wanted was to find bad guys. He needed that in his very soul, as a hound needs the chase. He was willing to accept almost anything as true, if it led him to the bad guys. Petersen *was* a poet, and a good one: published and polished. He hated the department knowing it. He barely forgave Giddy for letting the word slip.

But no matter. He went back to his threadbare office chair, to think. His propped feet left a large scuff on the windowsill.

"You *can't* go home," said Theodore once again, reasonably. "You can barely make it to the hall and back without support. "What will you do—sleep by the toilet and phone-in pizzas?"

"What's wrong with that as a lifestyle? Millions of Americans…"

"Can get off their butts if they need to. You, on the other hand, are not lazy but badly injured."

Ewen found himself in an obstinate mood. "I will not stay here one more day. I refuse. And I don't have the money to afford twenty-four-hour nursing care, so it's obvious I can just..."

"Go to *Sangye Menla*," Theodore finished for him. "It's perfect. It's meant to be."

Ewen swallowed what he had been about to say. "To a hospice? But Theo, the idea is that I'm *not* dying."

"Everyone is dying," said Theodore, with some ponderosity. "Dying every moment of their lives. And it's no big deal for you to stay there. We all know you, from when you do portraits."

"Dying every moment..." Wasn't that just Theodore? But even in his stubbornness, Ewen could think of no place else to go.

Had his brother-in-law not run a hospice, there would have been no chance of Ewen getting properly released, because of the severity of the wound and because many in the hospital felt a sense of ownership of this remarkable medical success. Theo, however, had taken from them many patients in worse shape than Ewen, and done well by them. As well as could be expected. Even the trauma specialist who felt Ewen's life was her own doing felt free to let him go.

The head nurse had her reservations. "Mr. Young—Ewen—you just have to remember you can't be using any of that judo any time soon."

"Judo?"

"No punching and kicking for at least a month, and I'd say two if I thought I had any chance of getting you to cooperate."

Ewen was leaning on the bed, trying to explain to the orderly which of the small pile of clothing he wanted to wear home. "You do me wrong, Mrs. Witherspoon. I've never felt less inclined to throw a kick in my life." He chose the green t-shirt. "Am I allowed at least to draw? Lying flat on my back, of course?"

"You can finger-paint for all I care," answered the head nurse. "Go ahead. Make a mess. And when you're on your feet again, I'll let you do a sketch of my bea-uutiful face!"

Ewen turned to her intently and then nodded. In her turn she blushed. "I didn't really mean it, Ewen. You know that."

"But I did."

Years ago, Ewen had begun his painting for *Sangye Menla* trying to make the works as peaceful and reassuring as he could, only to find that his wilder and more spontaneous sketches and painting were better received. As one man had said, "I'm dying. I don't have time for timid stuff."

Now there was very little timid stuff in the rooms of the dying. Ewen had once had no idea how pervasive a thing dying could be in the business of daily life until Lynn had married Theodore. In secret Ewen often referred to his brother-in-law as "The Tibetan Brother-in-Law of the Dead."

Over the years he had had to grow accustomed to his sister's devotion to the cause of the mentally and emotionally suffering, and the constant rotation in and out of their lives of the dying people in Theo's hospice.

Now he knew about it all in another way. Lying on a bed by the window with an Ellis Peters mystery book propped carefully on his body and a summer rain outside, Ewen wondered, somewhat uneasily, whether he ought to start conversations with the folks going about their business around him—tell them death wasn't so bad, once the pain stopped. Tell them not to turn their backs and spin away, as Chow had done. But he was embarrassed at the very idea.

That's what Theo talked about, and he did so at whatever length a person would listen. And Theo had studied it. He had the map of the place, and from Ewen's limited experience it seemed to be accurate. One patient, Francine Bellows, who was a middle-aged woman with bone cancer, had asked him how he was doing, but her words had seemed to Ewen more courteous than curious. He said he was doing fine. And he was.

But no kicking or punching for at least a month.

In Between

Sangye Menla was on the Ridge, outside the city of Redmond, a block from the Thurmonds' house. It lay in an acre carved out of the Douglas firs. It was very pretty, with red geraniums making splashes against the green shrubbery. Despite Ewen's warnings, Theo had planted a grove of black bamboo, shielding the hospice from the road. The bamboo seemed be behaving itself. On the front porch, outside Ewen's window and within easy eyeshot, was the terrible bonsai.

There were more nurse-practitioners than doctors working here, but today on-duty there was Willie Sherman, a special sort of doctor whom Ewen had once caught helping to change a bed. He could see and hear Willie across the hall, with his hawk-like face and hawk-like tenor voice, sharing a joke with someone just outside Ewen's sight. Ewen had discovered that Doctor Willie had come to the hospital the night after Ewen's surgery.

"Would have tried to get in on the operation if he'd known in time. Never seen such a wound. Would have been interesting." Dr. Willie talked in telegrams. He was too busy for nouns.

It was strange that Ewen had been catapulted over the border of life and death in time to meet Chow, but had failed to help his uncle. Of course he had been busy being shot at the time, but Ewen wished—if he had had the choice—to have assisted Uncle Jimmy. But maybe Uncle Jimmy hadn't needed any help. That was the better thought. Uncle Jimmy hadn't needed help. Not with the afterlife, at any rate.

Ewen's mystery novel fell back from his hands. He emitted a tiny groan and settled back to sleep.

Mr. Raymond Blundell was not hooked on cocaine. He could take it or leave it. Right now he chose to take it. He had certainly been pissed-off when he killed that moron Chow, but it wasn't the coke. No, it was sound business. He chose to snort another line. Now he had to write off the Young debt, of course, but that wasn't big time.

He had been a fool to hire a fool. Chow, with his stupid "fighting arts." It always came down to a gun in the end, so why bother with the middle? Blundell suddenly saw very clearly that he *wasn't* a fool after all, because how could he have known exactly how much of a moron Chow was? Even a Chinaman usually had more sense than to try intimidating a fighter in his own ring, as Chow had done to Young. That's just not gonna work. The guy's gonna fight. You're gonna have to use the gun, which was what made Chow the moron. Not Raymond Blundell.

With Chow, Blundell had done what he had to do. You can't leave a moron running around breathing with so much he could say about you. And say to anybody. Such as the police. Which is what a moron did, when they caught up with his moron ass.

Blundell was still pissed-off at Chow. He was now *really* pissed-off at the younger Young, because in spite of all Chow had said, Ewen Young was not spare parts; he had lived, and that was a stupid miracle. That was why Chow had to die. Blundell snorted another line and enjoyed being really pissed-off.

———

Gideon Ryde was trying to explain to Allie, his wife, what had happened at the hospital the day before. It was difficult, and in fact it couldn't be explained, so he had to trust Allie to see the truth beyond the impossibility. She didn't doubt Gid's veracity or his vision, but when he narrated what Theodore had said about the in-between, she looked not doubtful, but worried. "It sounds sort of...pagan?" she ventured.

Ryde sighed. "Well, I think it was pagan to a pagan, but that doesn't mean it was pagan in itself. It wasn't pagan to me."

Allie, who was a policeman's wife, said, "That'll do."

———

The next visitor was totally unexpected. For some reason, since being shot Ewen hadn't thought of his former live-in, Karen, at all. He felt instant guilt on the matter. She only lived in Tacoma, after all.

She walked in uncertainly, and sat on the edge of the bed, as beautiful and blond as ever. Paler than ever. "Ewen, forgive me, I was out of state. I only just heard."

"Forgive *you*? For what? I could have called. I should've. Forgive me for scaring you—I mean, if you were—"

"Scared? Out of my mind! I can't believe this happened to you, of all people. I guess it was that damn uncle of yours..."

"Enough of that," said Ewen, sharply, and then wondered why, once again, he was being backed into a corner defending Uncle Jimmy.

"I'm sorry, Ewen. It doesn't matter, anyway. The only thing that matters is that you get better."

Karen looked exactly the same. Ewen found he was wishing she'd changed her hair, at least. He felt he was trying to talk across a gap of two years and of two moments; He didn't know her at all, but at the same time he felt he could slide very quickly into the smooth intimacy of a couple that had lived together for three years. "I am getting better," he said. "Better every day. In a month I'll be on my feet again. No problem."

"But in the meantime," said Karen, diffidently, "If you need someone to take care of you...I could take some vacation..."

Ewen hated that phrase "take care of you." From Karen he hated it. "Aren't you still with Hugh?"

She hesitated. "Yes. Yes, more or less. But if you need me..."

"Thanks a lot, Karen, but I'm being taken care of up the old wazoo. It would be a shame for you to use up vacation time, and leave Hugh alone, when it's Theodore's pride and passion to hover over me. And then there's Lynn."

She sort of smiled. "Yes, there's always Lynn. You're 'two of a kind.'"

Things had gone too far, here, in just a few phrases. Too painfully far. "I'm really sorry, Karen. Forgive the way I'm talking. It's just the drugs they've got me on. I never know what I'll say next."

She took his hand in hers, impulsively. He almost flinched at the surprise of it, and at the memories. "But if you need anything, Ewen. Anything. Call me. The number's the same. I'll come running."

"Thanks, Karen," he said, and let his eyes droop, miming sleepiness. He heaved a great sigh. He heard her steps toward the door, and then: "Hey, Ewen. I hear you're doing really well. The painting business, I mean. Not about getting shot."

He mumbled something deliberately incoherent. "The painting business" indeed. That's what had really separated them. The painting business—which wasn't really a business at all, to Karen. That and the martial arts business. Ewen had been expected to go down in flames, because he rejected all Karen's serious advice. Karen, the department-store buyer. *Surprise, Karen!* He hadn't gone down in flames. He had done quite well.

He had only gotten shot in the heart.

Ewen found his drowsiness was not all invented. Perhaps not invented at all. Before he fell asleep he wondered what Mrs. Lowiscu, who sat like a sleeping snake, made of it all. Perhaps she was still sitting there, waiting.

Willie soared into the room, his hawk-nose lifted intently and his arms laden with sheets, which he dumped at the foot of the bed. "I see you had another visitor, Picasso. You'll have to start sending them to Mr. Parrish. He hasn't had a visitor all week. Now, though, we're going to get you up."

The "we" was only Willie, but the getting up was still brisk. The doctor got Ewen under one arm and heaved him to his feet. Those feet seemed to have forgotten the feel of weight on them. They tottered down the hall between selections of Ewen's own paintings, and he was not too proud to hold on to the doctor's elbow and hand.

Detective Rick Petersen had an informant who knew a lot about the business of gambling crime in King County. He told the detective that Chow was not a casino employee, but was connected to a big guy named Ray Blundell. "Blundell the bookie?" Petersen asked. "I haven't heard about him in a while."

Finerhan danced from foot to foot as he held out his hand to passers-by for spare change. Spare change-ing was not really his occupation: giving information was. But he didn't mind the spare change, either. "Blundell's no bookie. Not anymore. He bankrolls bookies. He bankrolls crack. Bankrolls all kinda stuff. Problem is, he's a cokehead himself. Makes him hard to work for, yaknow?"

Finerhan had graduated high school and finished a year of community college. He had once possessed all the words necessary for grammatical speech. One after another he had dropped them onto the streets and the sidewalks and never bent to pick them up again

"You used to work for him?" asked Petersen. "Blundell?"

Finerhan shrugged. "Naw. Notsomuch. But that's why he kill Chow. Pissed-off, yaknow? And, hey! Maybe that's why Chow kill Jimmy Young? Maybe he's on coke and pissed-off, too. Whatever, lissen to me: this stuff I'm givin' you is good and true. Blundell's your man and you gottawatch out, because he's a cokehead."

Petersen sighed, put his hand into his pocket, and gave the dancing Finerhan quite a bit of spare change.

Later that night all the spare change was gone, and Finerhan was feeling a bit ticked-off that Petersen hadn't given him more. It had been good and true information and Finerhan had deserved more. He told one of his connected bar buddies that the cops knew Blundell was connected to Chow, and they were gonna get him for the hit, which was all also good and true. Finerhan's business *was* giving information. He had enough sense remaining not to say it was he who had tipped the cops off. Instead he said that one of Jimmie Young's own people had figured it, which wasn't good and true, and in fact Finerhan didn't know who Jimmy Young's people were, or even if he had any, because Finerhan had never met Jimmy Young or even heard of him before this week. Still the information got him some more spare change. Finerhan knew he deserved it, and Finerhan was quite the cokehead too.

Doctor Willie was thinking about Mr. Parrish, who was shaking and cursing. It had been longer than one week, actually, since anyone had come to see the old man. Parrish was tough as nails. He was fighting death hard, and fighting his fellows harder. The nurses would only enter his room in pairs, fearing the strength of Parrish's still huge arms. So far he had thrown nothing heavier than a vase, but that had sailed quite far, and had Doctor Willie been the kind of guy to care about flying vases, or even flying bedpans, he would have exited the room by now. "Don't you want the pain medication, Thurgood?"

"Pain medication? You don't give me enough freakin' pain medication to do anything!" Parrish tried to rage, but ended up coughing instead. "I'm a big man. I've got big pain! I hurt like freakin' hell!"

Willie leaned against the wall, arms folded over his polo shirt. "But what *can* we give you if you keep tearing out your IV? Would you prefer constant needles?"

"I hate your freakin' needles. I already look like a mosquito masterpiece!"

From behind Doctor Willie, Ewen Young cleared his throat. "You know, doc, IVs have a habit of coming out by themselves." Ewen was leaning against the wall, but he was standing. By himself.

Parrish went on. "Just give me pills—two pills. Four. A dozen. Dammit, a shot of bourbon, already. Why do I have to live like I'm already dead, when..." He lost his train of thought, and his large, gaunt chest rose and fell like a bellows. "...when I just want something...Something."

Ewen slid past the doctor. He was staring with great concentration at Parrish and tilting his head slightly, as though he wanted to be sure exactly what he was seeing. Parrish looked up, still panting. "What're you lookin' at?"

Ewen only shook his head and kept staring. Parrish said "You're the guy..." Another spell of angry panting. "You're the guy they say died. Died and came back again."

"I guess that's what they say," said Ewen, distantly.

Parrish roused "Well that's crap. You're dead, you don't come back. You come back, you weren't dead. Got it?"

"Okay. Then I wasn't dead." Without invitation, Ewen sat down on the bed in the small space not taken up by the big man's frame. He crossed his legs and leaned slightly forward, touching Parrish's temple with one finger. There was a tiny crack in the air, as of static electricity, and Ewen pulled his finger back while Parrish glared at him.

"That a joke of some kind?" Parrish demanded. Ewen shook his head, stared some more, and then, more confidently, touched him again.

Doctor Willie watched, glad for any respite from the sound and fury. He saw Ewen's face tighten and watched as it seemed to age, while Parrish blinked and rubbed his eyes. Willie reminded himself that Ewen was a patient, too, and was probably more fragile right now than he looked. Perhaps more fragile than Parrish. He pushed away from the wall and stepped closer, only to see the two men sitting motionless, no longer touching. It seemed both Ewen and Parrish had fallen asleep. Then there was a shimmer in the doctor's vision, a loss of focus, and he could not clearly see the men on the bed. This loss of focus was a thing that happened to him frequently, working with the dying. Sometimes he developed a sudden allergy and had to blow his nose. Wipe his eyes. Distaining to take off his glasses, Doctor Willie merely squinted and the disturbance went away. He thought to wake Ewen quietly, to tell him to leave now that Parrish was sleeping. But he decided to let it be and went on his rounds.

Ten minutes later he saw Ewen leaning against the wall in the hallway, between two of his own paintings, breathing heavily. "You okay, Picasso? What did you do, put Mr. Parrish into a Yogic trance?"

Ewen looked very tired. "No. I don't know anything about trances, Doc. I just kept the boundaries. That's all I know how to do." Ewen walked carefully down the corridor to his own room, looking back once to say, "When he wakes up, I bet he's still gonna want his shot of bourbon."

"I'll tell the attending when I leave," answered Doctor Willie.

Young Teddy was leaning over the back of the sofa, which fronted the window, drumming his feet against the cushion beneath him. He was wishing he could go out, right now, into the sunshine, where his whiffle-ball and whiffle-bat were lying on the grass. He saw the blond detective stop his car and walk up the sidewalk to the door. Teddy waved exuberantly and ran to open the door. "Hi! Hello, Detective Ryyydde! We could go out and play and leave the grown-ups alone!"

Gideon Ryde took the hot little hand and smiled. "What grown-ups have we got today, Theodore?"

A door from the kitchen opened. "What's that? Teddy, you're not supposed to answer..."

"It's the Detective, Daddy. The one that wants to play with me." To Ryde he said, "We just got my daddy to come home. He's watching me. I can't do, like, *anything* anymore. But I could with you? I could with you?"

In sudden alarm Ryde remembered that he *had* suggested he take Teddy out to play. In other circumstances, of course. The tiny hand was locked on his like a limpet. Big Theodore entered the room, tall, bearded, slightly rumpled. "That's good it's Detective Ryde, son, but remember from now on to tell me first when someone comes to the door. Don't answer it."

Teddy was scornful. "Oh, it's not like they could get in! I'd be there!"

The two men locked eyes in perfect understanding. Ryde bent down. "Don't open the door for people, Theodore. Not even if you're sure they can't get in."

"Right," echoed Teddy's father.

Five minutes later, Theodore sat thoughtfully shaking his head. "No. The name Blundell doesn't mean a thing to me. Have you asked Lynn? She'd be more likely…"

"I know! I know! I know!" Teddy jumped up and down on the carpet, his too-long socks flopping in swags over his toes. Ryde glanced over at the boy.

"You know what, Theodore? Who is Blundell?"

Teddy stopped bouncing. He put his hand into his mouth. "I don't know," he said. Ryde stared intently, but Teddy said nothing more.

"He does that," said Big Theodore.

"Beg pardon?"

"Ever since school started he's had a bad case of the 'I knows.' Doesn't mean anything."

"Ah," said Ryde.

The next morning started badly for Ewen. When he woke up, even before heading to the bathroom, he glanced out the window to see one large branch of the bonsai was snapped, hanging like a broken arm along the trunk. He felt unreasonable panic. Stopping only to empty his bladder, he padded barefoot onto the porch and lifted the intricate little bough. It hung only by a strip of bark. If it could somehow be patched, he thought...Sewn back, like an amputated finger. But that wouldn't work; there was the phloem and xylem and whatever else that made a tree. He knelt on the wooden floor in his cheap blue hospice pajamas and bit his nails. "Oh no," he whispered. "Oh shit, oh shit. I'm done for."

Mrs. Swann was sitting there in a rocker. She hadn't slept well and had been there since dawn. "Well, young man, you must be very attached to that little tree."

"I hate it!" he blurted. "It's a white elephant!" Mrs. Swann merely rocked. "But it was a present, and took a long time to grow, and the guy will probably come looking for me..."

"Come looking for you?" she asked in some alarm.

"I mean come to see me, and he'll see this."

"Hide it," suggested Mrs. Swann, and Ewen thought for a moment.

He had never heard a more brilliant idea. "But hide it where?"

She rocked meditatively. "In the closet. Visitors here never look in the closet."

"But...there's no light in the closet. It'll die."

"You hate it," Mrs. Swann said reasonably.

Ewen decided to hide it in the closet. While he was toting the tree down the hall and it was both awkward and heavy, Mr. Parrish strode, rolling like a sailor on the deck, toward him. He was not wearing an IV. He stared at Ewen's burden. "That thing!" he spat. "I nearly broke my leg on it last night. It's dangerous."

"You broke the bonsai?" Ewen's voice shaded into menace. "You broke the bonsai? You admit it?"

"Hell! Damn thing nearly broke me!" Parrish's shoulders rose and his hands clenched. The two stared at each other along the length of the hallway like two gunfighters on a western street, both in blue pajamas.

Ewen spoke first. "Grab the other end of this," he said. They hid it in the closet.

Before stumping back to his room Mr. Parrish stopped and turned, as though he'd remembered something—as though he wanted to say something - but then stood silent, eyes narrowed, shaking his head slightly. He said "Oh, by the way, I guess if you complain loudly enough around here, you can get what you want."

Ewen made an interrogative, noncommittal sound.

"I finally got that shot of bourbon."

Dr. Young came by at eleven. They did not talk about his brother. They did not talk about the shooting. They talked only about the bonsai.

Ryan Watanabe came by at noon, and they talked about Uncle Jimmy's funeral, about seeing Jimmy's ex-wife, who had come up from Santa Barbara, and about how the school was holding together. It was a strained conversation, but then any conversation with Ryan was strained, as he was a creature of motion and not language. It was impossible to read what Ryan thought, except by the way he shot one fist into the opposite open palm. There was some emotion there: what kind Ewen could not be sure. Ryan took a lot of reading.

The tree was not mentioned, even in passing. Ewen did not trust this silence and he sweated. While Watanabe was still there, Detective Petersen showed up, which allowed Ewen to take leave of his fellow student. Police business and all. Watanabe left, uncertain himself what had been so odd about his visit. He never could read Ewen.

In fact, the tree had not been mentioned because his uncle's bonsai meant less than nothing to Ryan Watanabe. He didn't remember there was such a tree.

Detective Petersen was surprised at the warmth and excitement Ewen showed at his arrival, and wondered if perhaps Ewen Young had not had many visitors. That would have been a shame, since it seemed Young was a friendly sort of guy. Nonetheless, his voice as he spoke to Ewen was neutral, almost chilly. Petersen was a poet, but not a warm nor fuzzy one.

He told Ewen he was putting a car out in front of Lynn's house and was considering one outside of the hospice. "But since it's less than two blocks away, I was thinking we could make do with one. What'd you think, Mr. Young? You're an alert kind of guy. Will you let me know if someone or something feels wrong to you?"

Ewen stared hard. "A car at Lynn's? Now?" He stared, uncertain, and he thought. "What do you know today that you didn't know yesterday, detective?"

"Know? Nothing. I just get feelings, Mr. Young. Gut feelings. Considering what I've seen, you probably know all about gut feelings."

Ewen nodded and thought again. "One car should be enough."

As he walked out the door, Detective Petersen turned and asked how Ewen was feeling. "Alert," answered Ewen.

That evening Mrs. Swann went downhill. Everyone in the place knew this because of the number of family who came to visit. Ewen was sketching, trying to make as little noise as possible, when he was asked to visit her. This summons took him unexpectedly and his mood sank; he was tired and didn't want any more preternatural or even emotional experiences.

The number of people and the amount of worry in the room had made the air sour, but as Ewen pressed his way toward the bed, old Mrs. Swann had a smile for him. "Ewen! It's late to ask, but I would like you to draw me something."

"Sure," he said, "I'll just go get my stuff."

"Oh! I didn't mean of me. No. I meant of the tree. In the closet. Sketch the tree in the closet."

He stared, uncomprehending for just a moment, and then saw faint smiles on the faces of the Swann family. "She was just now talking about that tree," someone said. "The white elephant tree."

Ewen darted back and dragged the bonsai half out of the closet, catching the leaves on a pair of his jeans. Nothing broke. For fifteen minutes he sketched in charcoal, and in imagination he put the tree deep in the closet, its leaves still shining despite the darkness. He sprayed the sketch with fixative, got caught in the fumes, coughed, shook the sketch dry and ran back to Mrs. Swann's room. A woman in her fifties, maybe a daughter, held it out before Mrs. Swann's face, and the dying woman smiled again. "Thank you, Ewen," she said, and added, "May I keep it?"

He said, "Yes," meaning, as they both knew, "for as long as you can keep anything," and he backed out of the crowded room. He lay back on his own bed and hoped Mrs. Swann would have no other need of him, because he was very tired. He was already asleep when Mrs. Swann died. She had no further need of him.

Ewen peered out the window at the police car, which was barely visible. He was ready to get out of here. Living amongst the dying was just too much. It could just do you in. He worried he would become obsessed, like Theodore, or that he would become inured, like his father. He thought that thirty-two was too young to be living this way. He had some wild and crazy points left to use up, which had accumulated too long in his quiet life, and he wanted to spend them all. Today, if possible.

He put on his clothes—tight jeans and this time a red t-shirt, to show how young he really was, and how wild and crazy—and decided to tell them all he was going home. He felt so full of himself, or so frightened, that he tried to shadow-box for a couple of minutes, and then sat on the bed, heart pounding, feeling less energetic but equally uncomfortable about something or other. And feeling stubborn.

He was brushing his teeth when he got the call from his sister. It was not a call on the telephone. He spat into the sink, looked at his shocked face in the bathroom mirror, and said, "Oh crap."

In the hall he ran into Parrish—literally. The weight of the big man slammed him into the wall, but he kept his balance and tried again to run past. Parrish grabbed him by the arm and was dragged along.

"Lemme go. Lemme go," shouted Ewen. "Gotta go."

Parrish grinned. "Bathroom's that way," he said, but his expression changed as Ewen kept going, pulling Parrish along with him as a terrier pulls a tall man. "Whoa. Whoa, fella. Ain't you the guy with the hole in his heart?"

Ewen took a second to release the man's grasp, running backwards as he did so. "Not now! Let me go!" He took a huge, gasping breath and ran on, through the quiet lobby, where someone was packing up the last of Mrs. Swann's things, and into the door, which gave before him. He was in the lawn, on the driveway, and now realized his feet were bare. The gravel was slippery, but he did not feel its sharp edges. There was noise behind him, catching up.

Parrish hollered, "Where the hell we goin'?" Ewen didn't have breath to answer. His mind was clear, but it was a sort of swimmy-clear. It all had to do with his sister. Parrish had him by the arm again, but not to slow him down. "Where we goin'?" he shouted once more.

They were coming to the police car, which was parked halfway between the hospice and Lynn's house. The driver's side window on the car was shattered, and Ewen found himself stopping before it, looking in at the shattered head of the uniformed officer behind the wheel. In his ears an enormous drum was pounding, and for a second there were no thoughts, only the knowledge that the asphalt beneath his feet was very hot.

"Shit!" said Parrish, seeing the dead policeman. "Shit, goddam!"

Ewen started again toward his sister's house, first dragging Parrish with him, then, as the big man saw their destination, being dragged by him. "Shit!" said

Parrish again. "Shit, goddam." Ewen had no air to spare for speech.

There was the front garden, so much messier than that of the hospice. A whiffle-ball. A whiffle-bat. Teddy's plastic tricycle, lying on its side in high grass. The old rose bushes in which Ewen had once painted a blond man with his hand bleeding in the red roses: this man now dead. Up the peeling stairs he clambered to the door, which was locked. "I don't fuckin' believe you!" came a voice Ewen didn't recognize, followed by a slam against a wall. It was a noise too loud to have been made by Teddy's little frame, and too small to have been made by Theodore's. Ewen hadn't needed the sound to know what was happening. He stood with both hands pushing against the door, and then was pushed aside himself by Parrish, who threw his weight with huge commitment against the panels. Ewen knew the door, and its locks and hinges, and the state of his own strength. He had an idea, but was not sure it would work. "Goin' in!" he said, not particularly to Parrish or to anyone, and he disappeared from the porch.

"Goddam!" said Parrish, staring around himself. "Shit, goddam!"

Ewen was inside. He saw them all: Lynn, Theodore, and Teddy, but not as he was used to seeing them. They were brilliant in color—hurt and brilliant. Theodore was on the ground, bleeding brilliantly, but aware, and Lynn had slid down the wall, breaking the plaster. Her mind was concentrated like a beam of light upon her child.

Teddy shone like a young sun, with his hand in his mouth and his face swelling like a melon. In the middle of it all stood a man Ewen had never seen before, a big, heavy, red-faced man with an aura that looked like an ugly lava-lamp and a gun in his ugly hand. Ewen tried to knock the gun away, only to find he was not material and could not touch the thing.

"You are *not* living through this, bitch!" The ugly man waved the gun at Lynn and then at Teddy, and his ugly mind was whirling. The sight of him was nauseating to Ewen. He felt his own spirit sink within him and as it did so, he gained materiality and moved again. He now had enough body around him to confront the man, who must have been the one Petersen had called Blundell.

"You're the one not living through this!" Ewen shouted, and he punched the man in the throat. The blow was good—focused—but not as strong as he had expected. The huge sound of heart-pounding was back in his ears. It shook the room. Even Lynn, even Teddy, even the stunned mind of Theodore seemed to hear it, for they all turned toward it.

Blundell put his hand up to his neck, as though uncertain what had happened to him. His breath whistled and blood started to erupt from his nose and lips. His eyes focused upon the form of Ewen before him and he mumbled with loathing, "Oh, not you! The fucking cause of it all!" Blood spattered as he spoke, some of it landing on Ewen and some of it passing through him.

Ewen stored away the strangeness of that statement—that he was the cause of it all—thinking later it might be important. Later it might make sense. He struck at Blundell's gun hand again and this time succeeded in whipping the long arm in a circle. He was still not strong enough. He shouted, making little sound, and in his anger he willed to be back in the real world once again. To be physical amongst the physical once again.

The room was getting more real by the moment, but by the same moment he was also wearing out. Blundell, coughing and staggering, his breath wheezing around his cracked windpipe, aimed the gun on the form of little Teddy, who was curled in the corner, sucking on his hand. "One more move out of you, you fuck, and the kid comes apart."

"How will that help you?" Ewen cried, and he heard his voice coming from a distance. The big drum in his ears was getting louder as he solidified as he came down. Now Ewen was *there* enough to see that Blundell's face was beet-red, and his eyes were dry and starey. Drugs, thought Ewen. Coke? Meth? Ewen had no idea. But he knew that it didn't matter to this man that shooting Teddy wouldn't help him, or that shooting the cop hadn't helped him. There was no hope to be found in reason right now. Ewan leaped between Blundell and Teddy, but at that same moment Blundell himself turned away to follow the sound of the great drum. Everyone seemed to be listening to Ewen's heart-drum, and then the drum shattered the door off its hinges and it hadn't been his heart after all, but Mr. Parrish's fists, and Mr. Parrish staggered into the room.

The two big men were much of a match in size, but Parrish had cancer, whereas Blundell had a Beretta. They grappled for a moment and Blundell managed to aim the gun at Parrish. From behind, Ewen punched Blundell double-handed in the back, just as he had punched Chow the week before. Not even a week before. The gun went off into the wrecked door and then Blundell, brought to his knees, managed to right his aim. He shot again. Parrish went down, but he was dragging Blundell to the floor with him. The gun was hidden between the two men.

Ewen, completely real now and completely winded, leaped into the air and came down, adding his weight to the blow he struck Blundell in the back of the neck. More blood spat from the man's broken throat to his mouth. The gun went off again, turned back upon its owner, and Ewen witnessed Blundell's ugly lava-lamp spirit spinning away. He saw it retreat from the room down a dim passageway that had not existed before, and something in it called to him.

The in-between called to him.

Ewen turned away from it. He stepped over Blundell's body to Parrish, who was lying flat with a hole in his blue pajama top and a big, idiot grin over his face. His eyes met Ewen's. "Shit. Goddam! That was great, kid! That was just what I needed. Better than bourbon."

"It *was* great," Ewen answered. "Because of you, it was great."

Parrish gave him a nudge with one big fist. "Hell, it was great all around." The fist dropped and Parrish's light, too, retreated. Now Ewen followed after.

It was actually good to get away from his body this time, because that body was fairly used up, and Ewen had by now become almost accustomed to the ground luminosity. He knew what to do, what to say.

But to his immaterial surprise, he found he was someplace else. He was in the small place with the damp grass and the trees set around—the place that had been his only magic before this week's catastrophe—where off to one side there was a little stone wall, with a trickle of water flowing beyond it. He was in his own place, where he kept the boundaries but where his own feet had never stood before. There he stood, in the middle of his own fantasy. Mr. Parrish stood beside him, but not with a hole in his chest, and not in the hospice blue pajamas. Mr. Parrish was wearing Levis and a denim jacket, and he seemed in considerably better shape than he had been before. "Hey, hey! I know this place. Remember kid? I came here with you one time. Yesterday."

Ewen sighed. "I'm thirty-two years old, Mr. Parrish Not a kid. And, yes, I know this place. I made it."

Parrish looked only amused. "You made it? Who are you, God?" He started walking, his hiking boots swishing through the green grass.

"No. I mean I saw it once and I use it. For years I've used it. It's a place to go, and to take other people."

Parrish kept going. "So, then tell me—where are we? Where're we goin' this time? This time I don't feel like sitting like a lump."

Ewen walked behind him. "Where we *are* is a park near Santa Barbara, where I grew up. Where we're *going*, I have no idea."

"Santa Barbara. Santa Barbara. Never been to Santa Bar-bara. Sounds nice. But why here? Why'd you use this place?"

Again Ewen sighed. "Because I was a bummed-out teenager when I found it, that's why! Do I need a better reason?" There was much Ewen didn't want to say to Parrish, about his being a bummed-out teenager.

"And you were a real pissed-off son a bitch when you were a teenager, right?" Parrish was in a strong, good mood.

"Wrong," said Ewen, feeling really pissed-off at the memory. "Not a son of a bitch at all."

"Too bad," said Parrish, who had almost reached the edge of the ring of trees. "And what's on the other side, here?"

Ewen opened his immaterial mouth to say it was a cemetery; that he had spent his best teenage hours sketching in a cemetery, but he felt too embarrassed to speak. Parrish's big hand reached into the cedar trees and pushed aside the heavy foliage, but instead of the manicured lawn and the rows of flat headstones, laid like chocolates in a box, Ewen saw only more trees.

"Pretty good," said Parrish, and he reached down to pick up a backpack that hadn't been there before. "Looks like a big place. And I'm in the mood for something big, after all the candy-ass shit I've been goin' through." Something sloshed in Parrish's jacket pocket and Ewen saw it was a silver flask. Parrish stepped into the woods, his heavy boots pressing down the moss on a path Ewen had never seen before. "You comin'?"

Ewen peered into the cathedral forest, and thought *"The woods are lovely, dark and deep..."* but he was alive. He was thirty-two years old and he was alive. He shook his head.

Parrish did not seem surprised and did not encourage Ewen. He was tightening the strap on his pack. "Bye, kid. See you around," he said.

Ewen let go the boundaries once again, and found himself panting on the floor of Lynn's living room, watching his sister press a wad of cloth against Theodore's chest. Theodore was propped up against a wall, blinking, his gaze fixed on the face of his wide-eyed son. There were two dead men in the room, both of them large. There was the sound of a siren in the distance. Teddy flung himself against Ewen, shouting. "Uncle Ewen! Uncle Ewen!" His face was sadly swollen, but he was not crying. "Did you see what happened? Everything happened! Daddy got shot. A strange man came in and he got shot. And then another one! Did you see?"

"I saw," said Ewen. "I saw a lot."